The Unicorns vs. the Eights

Jessica cleared her throat loudly as the Eights passed by us. "Yeah, Brandon Blitzen called Elizabeth personally yesterday to ask us to be on the *Best Friends* show," she announced, tilting her head to make sure the Eights overheard her. Amanda stopped dead in her tracks, and so did her friends. "He wants us to be on the show as soon as possible," Jessica went on. "Right, Elizabeth?"

"Well . . ." I started to say. Jessica gave me this look as if to say, *Come on, Elizabeth, back me up on this!* "Actually, they called the second they got my letter." When I glanced over at Amanda, she was staring at me.

"Are you guys serious?"

"We're scheduled to appear next Thursday," Maria said. "Live and in person."

"Anyway, we'd love to tell you more, but we have to practice now," Lila said. "Come on, you guys. We still have a few minutes." She started walking toward the big oak tree in front of school.

"I think Amanda's worst nightmare just came true," Lila said as soon as we were out of earshot. "There's no way they can outdo us this time!"

Bantam Books in THE UNICORN CLUB series.
Ask your bookseller for the books you have missed.

Coming soon:

THE UNICORN CLUB

THE BEST FRIEND GAME

Written by
Alice Nicole Johansson

Created by
FRANCINE PASCAL

BANTAM BOOKS
NEW YORK • TORONTO • LONDON • SYDNEY • AUCKLAND

RL 4, 008-012

THE BEST FRIEND GAME
A Bantam Book / March 1994

*Sweet Valley High® and The Unicorn Club™
are trademarks of Francine Pascal*

Conceived by Francine Pascal

*Produced by Daniel Weiss Associates, Inc.
33 West 17th Street
New York, NY 10011*

Cover art by James Mathewuse

ISBN: 0-553-48210-6

Published simultaneously in the United States and Canada

Bantam Books are published by Bantam Books, a division of Bantam
Doubleday Dell Publishing Group, Inc. Its trademark, consisting of the
words "Bantam Books" and the portrayal of a rooster, is Registered in U.S.
Patent and Trademark Office and in other countries. Marca Registrada.
Bantam Books, 1540 Broadway, New York, New York 10036.

PRINTED IN THE UNITED STATES OF AMERICA

OPM   0 9 8 7 6 5 4 3 2 1

112729

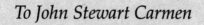

To John Stewart Carmen

One

My name's Elizabeth Wakefield. You've probably heard a lot about me. And if any of it was from my sister, it's absolutely not true. Jessica, my identical twin, is the hugest exaggerator in the world, and I'm not exaggerating.

(Sorry, Jessica. But you know it's true.)

For instance: I do like to read books, but I'm not the biggest bookworm on earth, although Jessica calls me that whenever she catches me curled up in bed reading a murder mystery novel. (My favorite.)

And I don't always get straight A's in school. I did get a B once. OK, so maybe that was five years ago, in second grade, but it still counts. Anyway, what's wrong with being smart? Nothing. It's just that Jessica can't stand it, because even though she's just as intelligent as I am, she never seems to do as well academically. Probably because she'd rather do anything but her homework on any given night.

As you can probably tell, Jessica and I aren't identical, really, except for our looks. We both have long, blond hair and blue-green eyes. The way people tell us apart is by the way we wear our hair: I usually put mine in a ponytail or in barrettes, and Jessica always wears her down around her shoulders.

But other than our looks, we're not very much alike, except for the fact that we're best friends, and we'd do anything for each other.

We're even members of the same club now—the Unicorn Club. I never thought I'd be a Unicorn, because last year the club was made up of some pretty snobby girls, and they pulled some stupid stunts. But this year something changed. It's as if when everyone hit the seventh grade, they started being a little more serious about things. Now the Unicorns do more than just have parties and dress all in purple—the club's official color—although we still do both of those things.

For instance, we volunteer at the Sweet Valley Child Care Center, a place that provides day care for parents who need it but can't afford to pay for it it. Actually, Maria and I have been volunteering there since last year, but everyone else just started when Mr. Clark, our school principal, sentenced the Unicorn Club to thirty hours of community service, because they'd been causing trouble at school. I know it must sound like working at the Center started off as a jail sentence or something, but it's really a blast, working with all the little kids. And a few weeks ago, we pitched in to cover some extra hours at Evie Kim's grandmother's thrift store. But we manage to have a lot of fun, too—we're not *that* serious.

Anyway, that Thursday afternoon we were at my house, having a meeting. We rotate our meetings, so they're at a different house every week. That way one person doesn't always get stuck cleaning up after we all sit around and get popcorn in between the couch cushions—and our parents don't go crazy, either.

Actually, the biggest problem with having the meeting at our house isn't my parents—it's my fifteen-year-old brother, Steven. He thinks the Unicorn Club should be outlawed. He says that all we do is sit around comparing brands of hair spray and collecting rock-star cards. He always manages to get in some crack about unicorns being phony, even though I've told him a hundred times they're mythical.

Anyway, the big thing we had to discuss that Thursday was a matter of utmost importance— well, not to us, but to Mr. Clark, our principal. A few weeks back we'd ruined his toupee. And he wasn't exactly enjoying being bald.

"He said that if we don't get him another hairpiece soon, he's going to have to consider banning us as a club again," Jessica told everyone.

"When did you see him?" Mandy Miller, our

president, asked. Mandy's most distinguishing characteristic is that she has the best wardrobe—and it's made up almost entirely of vintage clothing. I couldn't pull off wearing half the stuff she wears, because it's so funky and sometimes even weird, but she always looks fantastic.

"On my way out of school," Jessica said. "I suggested that, you know, he could sort of buy it for himself, and then we could pay him back."

"And what did he say?" asked Ellen Riteman. Ellen's been in the Unicorns forever, as long as Jessica and Lila. She has short brown hair and blue eyes.

Jessica cleared her throat and spoke in a low voice, imitating Mr. Clark. "That's not the point, Jessica. Certainly I could replace it myself, but the point is, you and the other Unicorns ruined it, and it is your responsibility to replace it." She frowned. "He actually said it was a matter of *principle*, can you believe that?"

I groaned. "Talk about a bad pun."

"We've got to come up with the money for that thing," Lila Fowler said. "Who would have guessed that a stupid toupee would cost three hundred dollars? I mean, Mr. Clark never looks *that* good."

Lila was right. Mr. Clark's fashion sense was about as good as my brother Steven's—nonexistent. Then again, his fake hair had looked pretty real. I'd never have guessed he had a toupee.

"So we need to either make a pile of money or

find some other way of getting Mr. Clark a new toupee," Evie Kim said. "We spent all the money we made working at the thrift store on paint for the lockers." First Jessica had painted a purple stripe down the South Hall lockers on a dare from Lila. Then, to paint over the stripe, she'd bought loud, bright pink paint instead of the industrial pink she was supposed to get. For some reason, whenever Jessica's in charge of a project, it has a tendency to turn into a bit of a disaster.

"We could . . . have a bake sale," Ellen suggested with a shrug. "It's worked before, right?"

"I have a better idea." Mandy held up her hair and pointed at Lila's long brown hair. "Let's cut off our hair and *make* him a toupee."

"No way!" Lila cried as everyone started laughing. She flipped her hair over her shoulder, the way she does about a hundred times a day. "Mr. Clark is not getting one strand of hair from me."

"Lighten up," Jessica said. "She was only kidding!"

Lila frowned. "Sure."

"What's with you today, anyway?" Maria Slater asked Lila. "You've been acting grumpy all afternoon. Did you max out on your dad's credit card or something?"

Lila's incredibly rich—or her father is, anyway. (Her parents are divorced.) She lives in a large mansion, has servants, and gets pretty much anything she wants. She even gets chauffeured around town in a Rolls-Royce limo, which is the nicest car I've ever seen.

"No, nothing as bad as that," Lila said. "It's just that I can't stop thinking about Amanda Harmon and her stupid club. Today had to be the tenth time this week that she started bragging to me about that big party she's having this weekend."

"Oh, you mean the absolutely huge one? To which none of us is invited?" Mary Wallace added. "She is pretty rude."

Amanda Harmon was the president of a new club at school called Eight Times Eight—the Eights, for short. The Eights were made up of eight eighth graders, and as far as I could tell, they were all pretty obnoxious. It's not that we had something against other clubs or thought ours was the only one that should exist or anything. It's just that it seemed Amanda and her friends were only doing things to compete with us lately. If we had a fund-raiser or a dance, the Eights had one, too—and they always tried to outdo us. It was bugging all of us, even me. And I'm not very competitive by nature.

"What's rude is how she thinks her party's going to be the best one ever in Sweet Valley," Lila grumbled. "I mean, come on. Everyone knows *I* throw the best parties."

I couldn't help smiling. Lila never misses a chance to remind everyone just how great she is. If there's ever a contest to decide who's most confident, she'll definitely win—and she'll also be the first person to predict she'll win. Lila's not exactly shy when it comes to promoting herself.

Lila and Jessica have been best friends for a long

time, and I used to wonder how Jessica put up with her. But now that I know Lila better, I can see that there's a lot more to her than just designer clothes, fancy jewelry, and a big ego. She's an incredibly loyal friend, even to me, and we haven't been friends that long. She uses her money for lots of good causes, too, like taking all the day-care kids to the zoo or buying clothes for the needy.

"Well, I'm sure her party won't be that great," Jessica predicted, obviously trying to cheer Lila up. "After all, *we* won't be there."

"True," Mandy agreed. "And if we're not there, there won't be any good dancers—"

"Not to mention good dressers," Ellen added. "I mean, really, what's the point of having a party without inviting us?"

Maybe I should have told you before—sometimes everyone gets a little carried away about being the best club in school. You've probably already noticed that. I don't necessarily think we're "the best"—as far as I'm concerned, there's no way to rate one club over another—but I do think we're great at being good friends to one another.

"Hey, isn't it time for that new game show?" Evie asked, pointing to the digital clock on our VCR.

Jessica grabbed the remote from the floor and pressed the channel button until she hit 32, a local cable station. It was four o'clock, and just as she turned up the volume, the theme for *Best Friends*, a new game show, started playing.

"I love this show—it's hilarious," Evie said, scooting her chair around to get a better view of the TV.

"Did you see those boys bomb out last week?" Mary asked. "They didn't even get *one* answer right."

"I know," I said. "I wonder how they even got on the show."

"They must have been desperate for contestants," Maria said with a shrug. Maria's done a lot of acting, both for TV and the movies, and she knows a lot about the entertainment world.

On *Best Friends*, groups of up to eight kids try to answer these wacky personal questions about one another. There are two teams who compete against each other, and the winners get prizes like school supplies, clothes, gift certificates to restaurants, even concert tickets sometimes. The show had only been on for a few months, but each one had been so hilarious, it already had a reputation for being a can't-miss show. The questions were sometimes off-the-wall, and the contestants would look completely stumped until they squeaked out some kind of answer. Sometimes people got into big, serious arguments over little things, like whether they were 5´4˝ or 5´5˝.

"Don't you think he's so cute?" Ellen asked, gazing at the show's host, who was grinning as he walked onto the stage to introduce the two teams.

"Yeah, for someone named Brandon Blitzen," Mandy joked.

"That can't be his real name," Maria said, laughing. "It's probably John Smith or Stanley Gluepepper or something."

Brandon Blitzen shook hands with all the contestants, then walked back to the little podium where he stood to ask the questions. The camera followed him, then zoomed in on his face. He was pretty handsome, even if he looked a little plastic, with his hair perfectly in place and a layer of stage makeup coating his face. Brandon grinned at both sides of the stage, at each team behind its little counter.

"And now, teams," he said, "it's time to find out the answer to the all-important question. Can you prove that you're really *best* friends?" He winked at the camera.

The small studio audience—about a hundred people—erupted into loud applause as the screen quickly dissolved to a commercial.

"That's it!" Lila suddenly cried.

"That's what?" I asked.

"That's how we'll do it!" Lila said. She was grinning. Her bad mood seemed to have evaporated.

"Lila, what are you talking about?" Maria said, shaking her head.

"All we need to do is to get chosen to be on this show," Lila said excitedly. "And then, voilà!"

"Voilà *what?*" Jessica asked.

"Amanda and the Eights won't have anything to hold over us anymore. If we get on *Best Friends*, we'll obviously win. Then we'll prove that we're the better club," Lila explained. "They'll never be able to top that."

"Plus, if we did win, there are a lot of good prizes," Ellen pointed out.

"Do you really think we could get on there? I bet lots of people try all the time," Mary said.

"They'll probably say something about how to become contestants," Jessica said. "Maybe we just have to send in a postcard or something. Let's watch."

Sure enough, when the show came back from a commercial break, the studio's address was printed on the screen, with the message "Become Contestants! Send us a letter and tell us all about you and *your* friends!"

Lila turned around, looked at me, and smiled. "All we have to do is write a letter. Piece of cake. Right, Elizabeth?"

"Yeah, if you write an essay about us and send it to them, we'll definitely get on the show," Jessica said, nodding eagerly at me. "They'll probably even ask us to come *twice*."

"Wait a second. How did *I* get recruited to write this letter?" I asked. "And what do you mean, an essay?"

"OK, a letter, then. You're only the best writer we know, Elizabeth," Maria said.

"Yeah, Elizabeth, you write all the time," Mary said. "You write for the *7 & 8 Gazette*, and then you write stories, and—"

"Come on, Elizabeth, you've got to do it," Lila

said. "You'll write them this prizewinning, absolutely awesome letter, and before you know it we'll be famous. Well, around Sweet Valley, anyway."

"Hey, we could even start the letter now, together," Evie said, pulling a notebook out of her backpack. "Maybe we can all think of ideas to help Elizabeth."

I sighed and grabbed a pen from the end table beside the couch. They were right: I do like to write, and I spend a lot of time doing it. Also, there was no point arguing with this group when they had their minds made up about something. I'd already found that out. "OK, what do you guys want me to say?" I asked.

"Put down that we're all extremely pretty and we'll look great on TV," Jessica volunteered.

"Yeah, their ratings are going to go way up," Ellen agreed, nodding.

I just looked at them and shook my head. A tiny local cable station probably didn't even *have* ratings. "We're supposed to tell them about us and why we're such good friends," I reminded everybody.

Jessica grinned. "I know. How about if you mention that your twin sister just happens to be gorgeous, and talented, and tell them how she's your very best friend and you'd do anything in the world for her—"

"Even write a letter all about her?" I interrupted.

"Right. Now you're catching on," Jessica said with a smile.

"And don't forget to mention that the Unicorn Club was my idea," Lila said. "Way back when. I mean, we wouldn't even be around if it weren't for me."

"I always thought it was Janet Howell's idea," I said.

"So? She's not in the club anymore, and anyway, I did help start the Unicorns," Lila huffed, obviously irritated that I'd mentioned her cousin, the Unicorns' former president, who was now in the ninth grade at Sweet Valley High School.

I could tell we weren't going to get very far, working this way. "How about if I write to them tonight?" I suggested. "I'll send the letter off tomorrow."

"OK, but make sure you mention how unbelievably interesting we are," Mandy said as Brandon Blitzen's face appeared back on the TV screen. "I mean, do they want a cool show or not?"

While Brandon asked the first question, I jotted down a quick note to myself: My best friends have to be the most overly confident people in the world! (Actually, it was a quality I really admired—except if someone got too cocky.)

But I thought if we could get onto the show, it would be a lot of fun. Especially if we won.

And how could we lose?

Two

Dear Mr. Blitzen . . . Dear Brandon . . . Dear Sir or Madam . . . To Whom It May Concern . . .

I folded up my eighteenth sheet of paper and tossed it under my desk, into the basket where I put stuff to go to the recycling program. It was Thursday night, and I'd been trying to write the letter for the past half hour, but I couldn't even figure out how to start it. If I wanted to write the letter without using up a whole tree, I was going to have to come up with some good ideas soon.

Focus, I told myself. *Just think about what makes all the Unicorns such good friends.* I tapped my pen against my desk, then began to write.

Dear Mr. Blitzen,
My friends and I have been watching your show ever since it came on, and we

think it's terrific. Actually, we think it's the best show on TV right now.

(I figured it couldn't hurt to butter him up a little.)

There are eight of us, and we have a club called the Unicorn Club. We all attend Sweet Valley Middle School. Let me tell you about each of us:

First there's my twin sister Jessica, who'd get mad if she found out I talked about anyone besides her first. Jessica's always been my best friend, which is pretty incredible if you know us, even though it might seem obvious since we're twins. We don't always agree on things—actually, we're incredibly different—but I know Jessica would do anything in the world for me, even if it was really dangerous or hard. (I don't know if she'd give up watching her favorite soap opera, *Days of Turmoil*, even for me. I guess I'd better hope I never have an emergency between three and four in the afternoon.)

Lila Fowler is Jessica's best friend (besides me, that is). Lila's father is very rich, so Lila lives in a huge house. She likes music and dancing, and she recently made friends with a little girl named Ellie at the Sweet Valley Child Care Center, where we all volunteer. They really hit it off, which surprised me because I always thought Lila was too selfish to be interested in helping a little kid like Ellie. But they really seem to like each other.

Mandy Miller's the president of the Unicorns. I really like Mandy because she always has something funny to say and always tries to cheer other people up, even though she might be having a lousy day herself. I guess because she had cancer last year, she has kind of a good perspective on life: you can't take it too seriously. Mandy shops at thrift stores constantly and makes up the coolest, most original outfits. I think she'd make a great fashion designer someday.

Sometimes she helps Evie Kim, another Unicorn, down at the vintage clothing store that Evie's grandmother owns. Evie just moved to town—she's a year younger than most of us, and she's Asian. Evie plays the violin beautifully. Back in Los Angeles, where she used to live, Evie knew Maria Slater, another Unicorn. (Have you lost track yet? I hope this isn't too confusing.) Maria was a child actress who did movies and TV commercials. In fact, she just finished filming a movie here in town. Her part's really small, but it was fun because we all got involved as extras. I can't wait to see that movie when it comes out. Anyway, Maria's very pretty, with dark, wavy brown hair and medium brown skin.

I've known Mary Wallace since we were little kids, and the best thing about Mary, even though it might sound boring, is that she's *extremely* dependable. That's why she's the treasurer of our club. Mary's a little on the preppie side, and she was a foster child until the family she's living with now adopted her. Mary's really fun to be around, too.

Then there's Ellen Riteman, the seventh Unicorn. (Still with me?) Ellen's kind of a gossip, but she doesn't mean it in a bad way. She just doesn't think sometimes. And other times she'll surprise you by doing something incredibly thoughtful. Like the day I had a really hard Spanish test, and she brought a package of tortilla chips to help me get into the mood. Ellen's pretty funny sometimes, too.

Last of all, there's me, Elizabeth Wakefield. I got chosen to write this letter because I love to write. I'm a reporter for our school newspaper, plus I write short stories, too. Everyone thinks I'm going to be a famous writer someday, like my favorite mystery novel author, Amanda Howard. But I don't care whether I ever get famous. I just like doing it.

We'd really appreciate it if you'd consider having us on your show as contestants. We know a lot about one another, maybe everything there is to know! I'd say the three following characteristics make us perfect for your show: (1) we're not shy, (2) we can be very entertaining, and (3) we know what it means to be "best friends." I think friends are one of the most important things in life. My friends are always there for me when I need them, and vice versa. I can rely on them for anything, and sometimes, when I least expect it, one of them does something so nice I can hardly believe it. I'd never make it through junior high if it weren't for them.

We hope you'll decide to have us for contestants. In the meantime, have fun doing the show—we'll be watching you!

Sincerely yours,
Elizabeth Wakefield

I put my address and phone number at the bottom of the letter. When I read it over, I decided it was good enough. Besides, it was after nine o'clock, and I needed to get ready for bed. I put the letter in an envelope and sealed it.

I had just changed into my nightgown when Jessica came into my room. "Did you write it yet?" she asked.

I nodded. "It took me a while, but I finally did it."

"Let me see it!" Jessica walked toward my desk. "Is this it?" She picked up the envelope. "Hey, no fair—you already sealed it."

"Sorry," I said. "You'll just have to trust me."

"Well, did you tell him that he absolutely has to let us be on the show?" Jessica asked.

"Mmm . . . kind of," I said. "Not in so many words, but I think I got the point across." Jessica wasn't one to be subtle—if she'd written the letter, she would have demanded that Brandon Blitzen call her personally the second he got it.

"Good." Jessica walked over to my closet and started going through my clothes. "I wonder what I should wear when we go on TV."

"Don't spend too much time thinking about it. I mean, we might not even get—"

"Elizabeth! I thought you said your letter was good!"

"It is, but—"

"But nothing. You have to think more positively about these things. If we think we'll get on the show, then we will. *If* we really concentrate. I'll start by sending Brandon Blitzen some ESP messages." She closed her eyes and began to hum.

Jessica has this thing about ESP, strange occurrences, horoscopes—she really believes in all that stuff. I don't try to talk her out of it anymore, even though personally I didn't think trying to communicate with Brandon Blitzen by mental telepathy stood much of a chance.

I spent Friday afternoon over at the day-care center, where we all help out watching the kids now and then. Sweet Valley has a huge resource center for low-income families, and day care is just one of the things the center provides. Parents can drop their kids off all day while they're at work or looking for a job.

I've been volunteering there for about a year, and I'm really attached to the kids, especially one of them, Allison Meyer, who's five and has blond hair and big blue eyes. Allison has a twin sister, Sandy, and I guess sometimes the two of them remind me of me and Jessica when we were little. Allison and Sandy aren't much alike, either.

I even like the kids when they're being completely obnoxious, as they were today. I was glad that Mary and Ellen had come with me. At least with three of us we stood a chance. You see, the kids always get really hyper on Friday afternoons—in anticipation of the weekend with their parents, I guess.

Allison was doing some finger painting with Yuky, a Korean-American girl she likes to play with. Arthur Foo was running around the room, chasing Oliver, an African-American boy Jessica usually looks after. Ellie McMillan, the little girl Lila befriended, wasn't at the Center that afternoon.

"Allie, try to keep the paint on the paper, OK?" I suggested, as she wiped her hands all over her white smock. (Well, it *was* white fifteen minutes ago.)

Oliver stopped running and skidded across the floor until he bumped into me. "Where's Jessica?" he demanded.

"She couldn't come today, but she said she'd try to get here Monday," I told him.

"Oh." His face fell.

"Hey, you know what, Oliver? Jessica and I were talking about maybe taking all you guys to a football game at school next weekend," I said. "Would you like—"

"Yeah!" Oliver and Arthur yelled at the same time, before I even got out all of the question.

"What about you guys?" I asked Allison and Yuky, who had just managed to get streaks of yellow finger paint in their hair. I was glad the container said it was washable. "Do you want to come?"

"Yes," Allison said, nodding as she drew another swirl on the big poster she and Yuky were making. "Do we get to see the cheerleaders?"

"Who cares about that?" Yuky said, frowning. "I want to catch the ball!"

"Look at what I got for Mr. Clark!" Ellen held up a videotape. It was Monday morning, and we were standing by our lockers getting our stuff together for school. "This is the answer to all his problems."

"Must be a pretty long tape," Mandy joked. "What does it have on it, a complete makeover kit and guide to a happy life?"

"What is it?" I asked.

"Didn't I tell you guys? I sent away for it last week, after I saw an ad on TV. It's all about hair loss and what you can do to rebuild a thick head of hair *naturally*," Ellen said. "It was practically free, so I figured, why not? It might work."

"Did you watch it?" Lila asked.

"No, I didn't have time," Ellen said. "Besides, I wanted to give it to Mr. Clark all wrapped up, so he'd think it was expensive. Nobody wants a previewed tape."

"Especially not when they're expecting a hairpiece," I said. "Don't you think he's going to be a little disappointed?"

"Relax, Elizabeth." Mandy put her arm around my shoulder, and we walked down toward Mr. Clark's office together. "All Mr. C. wants to know is that we're trying, that we're thinking about him, and that we intend to make good on our promise."

We were halfway to Mr. Clark's office when we saw Amanda Harmon, the president of the Eights. (They gave themselves the nickname the Great Eights, but Jessica calls them the Crazy Eights.) She was standing with the rest of the girls in the club. I didn't know any of them very well, partly because they were too snobby to even talk to me when I tried to say hello to them. I had given up a few weeks ago, which is strange for me, because I can usually get along with anybody if I try. But in all the time I've been going to school with them, Amanda and her friends haven't ever bothered to be nice to me—or anyone besides themselves, as far as I could see.

Just as we were passing by the Eights—each group was so big, it kind of reminded me of two football teams getting ready to play each other—Amanda turned around to face us. "Well, if it isn't the Pretty Ponies," she said, with a phony smile.

"And this must be the Eight Times Zero Club," Lila said. "Multiply any number by zero and what do you get?"

I kind of cringed when I heard them talking like that. I didn't think things were *that* bad between us, but I guess Amanda and Lila really had a problem getting along. I tried to smile at Julia Abbott, to show her I didn't really hold anything against her club, but she just stared at me as if I weren't even there.

"Too bad you guys missed my party on Saturday," Amanda said, flipping her curly blond hair over her shoulder.

"Yeah, we had a great time," Marcy Becker added. "*Everyone* was there: Peter Jeffries, Rick Hunter, Caroline Pearce . . ."

"I can't wait to see the pictures you took, Amanda. I bet they're going to be great," Julia said. She turned to us. "Amanda's house was so packed, half the people had to stand outside on the lawn."

"It was probably a lot more fun outside—away from her," Mandy said to me under her breath.

"What did you guys do all weekend?" Amanda asked.

Jessica cleared her throat. "Oh, not much. We only practiced for our upcoming television appearance."

"Your *what?*" Julia asked.

"We're going to be on television," Jessica said.

I stared at her, hoping she would catch my eye. *Not yet we're not!* I wanted to say. Brandon Blitzen probably hadn't even gotten my letter yet, never mind asked us to be contestants on his show. But that was Jessica for you: always one step ahead of everything, even when she shouldn't be.

"Yeah," Lila said. "In fact, they practically *begged* us to come."

"Oh, are they having that phone-a-thon again, to raise money for the station?" Amanda asked. "I get it. You guys are going to sit there and answer the phones, right?" She and her friends giggled.

Lila gave her an arch look. "Hardly."

"We're going to be on *Best Friends*, which is only the coolest show on TV," Jessica announced, as confidently as if she'd signed the contract with Brandon herself. "Any day now."

"What? You can't be serious," Amanda said.

"Well, we are," Lila told her. "And you know what else? We're going to win—big."

Stop bragging so much! I wanted to say. I'd only mailed the letter a few days ago, and Jessica and Lila already had us walking away with the winners' prize.

Fortunately, the bell rang, and we all had to hurry off to our classes. "I'll drop the video in Mr. Clark's mailbox," Ellen called as she walked away. "Then we won't have to worry about finding any hair for him!"

I wasn't so sure about that. What was he going to do, wear the tape as a hat?

Three

I had just walked in the door after school on Tuesday afternoon when the telephone rang. I thought it was probably Maria, calling to see if I wanted to study for our science quiz together, the way we'd talked about doing.

"Hello?" I said.

"Yes, hello, may I speak with . . . hold on a second . . . Elizabeth Wakefield, please?" an older-sounding man asked politely.

"This is Elizabeth," I said. I felt my heart start beating a little faster.

"Hello, this is Dan Peterson," the man on the other end of the phone said. "How are you today, Elizabeth?"

"Umm . . . fine," I said. *Who is this guy?* I wondered.

"That's just great. Elizabeth, I'm calling with

some exciting news," he went on. I started to think he was trying to sell encyclopedias or a new long-distance phone service or something. I kept waiting for him to launch into his sales pitch. "I'm sitting here holding your letter," he said. "And I want to let you know how much all of us down here at Vista Vision enjoyed reading about you and your friends."

"Vista Vision? You mean Channel Thirty-two?" I asked.

"That's us," Dan said. "And it is my personal pleasure to invite you and your seven friends down to the studio to appear as contestants on *Best Friends*."

"Yes!" I screamed into the phone. I took a deep breath. "I mean, um, thanks."

"No, thank *you*," Dan said.

I rolled my eyes. His phony manner was actually starting to get on my nerves a little bit. "So did Mr. Blitzen like the letter?" I asked.

"Sure did," Dan said. "In fact, he loved it so much he'd like to get you on the show right away. Let me see . . . how does next Thursday sound?"

"Next *Thursday*? You mean, a week and a half from now?" I looked at the calendar beside the refrigerator. I couldn't believe it. I didn't know if we were going to be ready in time.

"That's right, Thursday the seventeenth. Of course, if you can't make it—"

"No, we can make it," I said right away. "We'll definitely be there!" I didn't know how, but one way or another we'd be there, prepared to win. Of course, we'd have to study nonstop from the second I got off the phone until—

Wait a second, I told myself. *What are you thinking? We don't need to practice—we already know each other inside and out!*

I called everyone that night to tell them the big news. Ellen screamed so loud, I thought I was going to go deaf in my left ear. Lila started talking about how she was going to do her hair and how she wanted to tape the show so she could send copies of it to all her relatives. Right away Mandy made plans for us to practice answering questions, starting before school the next day. And Jessica kept me awake half the night, talking about how this was going to be the start of something big.

"First we're extras in the movie, then we show up on a game show . . ." Jessica said dreamily, lying across my bed in her pajamas. "Talk about good acting experience. We'll probably be spotted on TV by some director and then—"

"Jessica, it's Channel Thirty-two," I reminded her. "The only time anyone watches it is—"

"During *Best Friends*," she said. "I mean, that's when everyone we know watches it, right?"

"True," I agreed. "But I doubt any talent scouts or agents are going to watch *Best Friends* in search of major Oscar material."

"You never know," Jessica said. "Anyway, we might at least get our picture in the *Tribune* if we win—I mean, *when* we win."

I punched my pillows and leaned back against them. "I wonder who we'll be up against. Maybe it won't be as easy as we think."

"What? Don't tell me you actually think we might lose," Jessica said, looking as horrified as if I'd just told her school was going to run through July instead of June this year.

"Not really," I said. "But all the contestants can't be as bad as some of the ones we've seen."

"We'll probably be up against some boys' soccer team or something," Jessica predicted. "They won't know anything except how many goals each one scored, or whether their favorite video game is Megamortal or Trompmeister."

I laughed. "If we're lucky."

"Luck has nothing to do with it," Jessica said. "Just skill. I can't wait for Brandon Blitzen to try to stump me with some question about *you*. It's going to be hilarious. We'll get so many points they'll have to add an extra column to the scoreboard."

What was it I said about having tons of confidence? But Jessica was right. How can anyone know someone better than her identical twin? I knew so much about Jessica, half the time I could tell what she was going to say before she even said it. I'd predicted what she was going to be for Halloween the past three years. I knew every crush she'd ever had, which music was her favorite, what games she liked—I even knew that she had bad dreams if she went to bed with a full stomach. Proving we were best friends was going to be a breeze.

*   *   *

On Wednesday morning, we'd agreed to meet out in front of school half an hour earlier than usual to practice. (Mandy had set up a schedule.) Jessica and I usually ride our bicycles to school, and I'm always waiting for her to get ready in the morning, because she takes twice as long as I do to get dressed. Half the time I have to wake her up, because she falls back to sleep after turning off her alarm.

But this morning, she was up even before I was. "What's gotten into you?" I asked. "Except for when you had to paint lockers at five in the morning so you'd be done before everyone got to school, you haven't been up this early in years."

"I can't *wait* to get to school," Jessica said excitedly.

"What?" I thought I must be hearing things.

Jessica grinned. "Wait until we tell the Eights that we're going to be on TV next week. I can just imagine the look on Amanda's face. She's going to explode."

I'd never seen Jessica ride her bike so fast before. Did I mention that along with being confident, Jessica's just a *tiny* bit competitive?

"So how should we do this?" Mandy asked once everyone had shown up outside school. We were all standing on the front steps. "What's the best way?"

"I think we should just ask whatever questions

pop into our heads, you know, and try to stump the other person," Ellen said. She took a bite of a muffin she'd brought with her.

We all looked at her. Not to be mean or anything, but Ellen isn't always known for having the brightest ideas.

"We're trying to find out stuff about one another, not the other way around," Mary said. "I mean, it won't really help us if we don't know the answers."

Ellen shrugged. "It was just a suggestion."

"We should make up descriptions of ourselves. You know, like people do when they're looking for jobs," Evie said.

"You mean a résumé?" I asked.

Evie nodded. "Yeah. We can put down all our vital statistics, like our birthdays, our favorite bands—"

"But we know all that already," Lila said. "What's the point?"

"It can't hurt to practice," I said. "You never know what they're going to ask us."

"Yeah, the last thing we want is to get asked something really obvious and not know the answer," Maria said. "We'll look like complete fools."

"Not a chance," Mary said. "It's too bad *Best Friends* isn't one of those shows where you get to stay on the show as long as you keep winning. You know, and get to be, like, grand champions?"

"Grand champions . . . it *does* sound like us," Lila said, and we all laughed.

"Look out—here come the Crazy Eights," Evie warned in a whisper. Amanda, Julia, and Marcy were headed toward us. They were wearing identical outfits: blue jeans, plaid shirts, and black shoes.

"Nice and original, huh?" Mandy eyed them critically. "That must be one of the club laws, that you have to buy all the same clothes."

"At least we only try to wear a little of the same color," Lila said.

"Even their hair is all the same," Maria observed. She was right—all three of them wore their long, wavy hair tied back in a tight ponytail with a plaid scrunchie.

Jessica cleared her throat loudly as they passed by us. "Yeah, Brandon Blitzen called Elizabeth *personally* yesterday to ask us to be on the show," she announced, tilting her head to be sure the Eights overheard her. Amanda stopped dead in her tracks, and so did her friends. "He wants us to be there right away. Actually, his whole staff does," Jessica went on. "Right, Elizabeth?"

"Well . . ." I started to say, but Jessica gave me this look, like *Come on, Elizabeth, back me up on this!* So I said, "Jessica's right. They called us the second they got the letter." When I glanced over at Amanda, she was staring at me.

"Are you guys serious?" she asked me.

"Serious about what?" Lila asked casually.

"About being on *Best Friends*," Amanda said. "You're really going to be on the show?"

"Would we say we were if we weren't?" Jessica retorted.

Amanda looked hesitant, as if she didn't know whether to believe Jessica.

"We're scheduled to appear a week from Thursday," Maria said. "Live and in person."

"Anyway, we'd love to tell you more, but we have to practice now," Lila said. "Come on, you guys, we still have a few minutes." She started walking toward the big oak tree in front of school.

"I wonder if they'll give us gift certificates to that new jeans store in the mall," Mandy mused as we walked off, leaving Amanda, Julia, and Marcy just standing there on the steps, in shock.

"Did you see the looks on their faces?" Ellen asked as soon as we were out of earshot. She was laughing so hard, she could barely get the words out.

"I think Amanda's worst nightmare just came true," Lila said. "There's no way they can outdo us this time."

I had no doubt that by the end of the day the word would be all over school that we were going to be on *Best Friends*. It made me kind of nervous, thinking of all the people who would probably be watching us. I'd never been on live television—or any television, for that matter. But at least I wouldn't be by myself. In fact, with Lila and Jessica around, I'd be lucky if I got a word in edgewise.

"Look at what I got from Mr. Clark." Ellen held

out a note typed on Sweet Valley Middle School stationery. She had just walked into English class, which we have together, and it was right before the final bell.

Ellen looked so worried, I knew it wasn't a thank-you note for the video she'd given Mr. Clark the day before.

"Dear Ms. Riteman and members of the Unicorn Club," the letter began. "I do not find your latest effort to replace my property commendable, nor in the least acceptable. This issue is by no means settled. I am still waiting, and you know to what I am referring." It was signed simply, "Mr. Clark."

"He can't even say the word *toupee*," I observed with a smile. "I guess he really doesn't like being bald."

"Elizabeth! I'm in big trouble, and that's all you can say?" Ellen replied. "I've never gotten a personal note from a principal before. What if he writes to my parents? What if he calls them today? What if—"

"Ellen, he's not going to do that," I assured her. "Mr. Clark's a pretty reasonable guy."

"That's easy for you to say. He *likes* you. I was just trying to get us out of trouble, and now I'm in even worse trouble than I was before," Ellen complained.

"Look, don't worry. We'll figure out some other way to get his hair back," I said. "I don't know how, but we will."

Ellen didn't look reassured. I guess if I had been

in her shoes, I wouldn't have felt so hot, either.

"Just remember, we're all in this together," I reminded her as the bell rang. "We'll find another solution."

"Give me the yellow pages and I'll look," Maria volunteered. "There has to be *someone* in Sweet Valley who makes cut-rate hairpieces that look like the real thing." Mandy handed her the phone book, and Maria started flipping through it. We had gotten together at Mandy's house after school for our first official *Best Friends* practice session.

"I'll look in my dad's favorite magazine to see if there are any ads in there," Mandy said, picking up a copy of *Man's World* from the coffee table.

"Couldn't we just call 1-800-NEW-HAIR or something?" Lila asked.

"Personally, I think Mr. Clark looks better without hair," Evie said. "I mean, what's so bad about being bald? There are millions of men who are— and a lot of them are even handsome."

"Maybe someone should tell him he looks better this way," Jessica said.

"You go ahead," Ellen scoffed. "*I'm* not going to. He hates me enough already."

I shrugged. "He doesn't hate you. He just didn't appreciate the advice on the tape, that's all. I don't think he'd appreciate advice from any of us right now."

"Wait a second!" Mandy held up the magazine she'd been leafing through. "Check this out!" She pointed to an ad on the side of the page.

"TIRED OF THAT BALD SPOT?" the headline said in big letters. "Cover it up—for only $7.95 a week!"

"What is it?" Ellen asked eagerly.

"It's this hair spray, only instead of being clear, it's the color of your hair," Mandy explained. "You spray it on your head and it looks like hair!"

Jessica started laughing. "You mean like spray paint?"

"Let's get him some spring green, or maybe a neon pink," Lila added, laughing.

"You guys, I'm serious! I've seen this advertised on TV, too," Mandy said. "Once they spray it on, it really looks like your natural hair. It comes in all different shades of brown, blond—"

"But Mandy, Mr. Clark doesn't have a bald *spot*—he has an almost completely bald head," Mary pointed out. "Would it still work?"

Mandy shrugged. "It's worth a shot. I mean, for seven ninety-five, how can we go wrong?"

"You order it, and we'll practice some questions while you're calling," Lila instructed. Even though she's not the president, sometimes she really acts like it.

"Elizabeth, where's that list of questions we wrote up last night?" Jessica asked me. She and I had spent half an hour trying to remember what kind of questions Brandon usually asked.

I took out my blank book, which I sometimes use for notes and sometimes use as a journal. I try to write in my journal at least three times a week, even if it's nothing very creative or exciting. I opened it to the right page. "OK. First, we thought we should all know each other's favorite foods."

"That's easy," Maria said. "Let me see . . . Elizabeth, yours is pineapple upside-down cake, ever since you had to make it in cooking class last year."

I smiled. "Right."

"Jessica, you love chocolate mousse. Ellen, you like banana-chocolate-chip ice cream at Casey's," Maria went on.

"Maybe the category should be favorite desserts," I joked.

"No, because *Lila's* favorite food is pesto spinach pizza," Maria declared.

"This is making me kind of hungry," Jessica said. "Hey, Mandy, do you have anything to eat?"

"Shhh," Mandy whispered. "Yes, that's right. Two-day express delivery would be great," she said into the phone. "Thank you very much!" She replaced the receiver and smiled at the rest of us. "It's a done deal. A can of Stanley's Super Spray is on its way!"

"What color did you get Mr. Clark—clear?" Jessica joked. "So he can make his head extra shiny?"

"No, it's called Medium Manly Brown," Mandy said, and we all cracked up laughing.

Four

Thursday morning, Jessica and I spent ten minutes at breakfast using flash cards we'd made up to grill each other on the other Unicorns.

"And who is my most favoritest dream date of them all?" Steven, my older brother, mimicked in a sappy voice, sitting down at the table carrying a bowl full of granola. (Ever since last year, he's been on this phony health kick, where he eats all healthy vegetarian food one day, and all junk food the next.)

"Not you, that's for sure," Jessica said, frowning at him.

"So do you two think you'll be ready by next week?" my father asked us, intervening as usual between Jessica and Steven. Once they start arguing, it can get pretty ugly. Especially first thing in the morning, when they're not in the best mood.

"I still can't believe you're going to be on TV," my mother said. "We'll have to tape the show so we can send a copy to your grandparents."

"Not to mention the TV Hall of Fame," Jessica said.

"Yeah, for worst performance ever," Steven joked.

"We're going to be great," I said, ignoring him. "I mean, maybe we won't get every question right, but we do know a lot about one another."

"I'll say," my father commented, as he buttered a piece of toast. "You've all been such good friends for so long, I'll bet you know more about each other than just about anyone."

"Are you guys going to come watch the show live?" I asked.

"Already asked for the time off," my mother said. She's an interior designer, and my dad's a lawyer. They both work long hours, but they try to make time for special occasions, and even some not-so-special ones.

"That's great," Jessica said, grinning. "You have to promise to cheer really loud, OK?"

"Oh, we will," my father said. "Trust us."

"What about you, Steven? Are you coming to the studio?" I asked.

He shrugged and took a sip of orange juice. "If I have time."

"Oh, like you're *so* busy," Jessica said. "Come on, Steven. We'd go and cheer you on if you were on a quiz show. Why don't you get a bunch of your friends to come, and you can make a lot of noise."

"Yeah, but if you do decide to come, make sure you're cheering for us, not heckling us," I said.

"You know what? I think I will come," Steven said, suddenly seeming excited about the idea. "Maybe the camera will pan the audience, and I'll be on TV. Then all my friends will see me, and it'll be totally cool."

I just looked at Jessica and rolled my eyes. Trust Steven to turn our TV appearance into an opportunity for him to look cool.

"Maria's a Capricorn, Ellen's a Pisces, Mary's a Gemini—"

"Aries," Mary corrected Evie. She took a sandwich out of her lunch bag and unwrapped it. It was Thursday at noon, and we were in the cafeteria. I guess I don't need to tell you what we were doing.

I felt sorry for Evie. We'd only gotten to know her about a month ago, and she had a lot to learn about all of us. But then again, I hadn't exactly been best friends with Lila for years, either—I was still finding out stuff I hadn't known about her, too.

"OK." Evie jotted down Mary's name on her napkin, then drew a picture of a ram next to it. "Using a picture helps me remember better," she explained. "All right, let me think for a second. Lila, you're a Leo. And Jessica and Elizabeth, your birthday's in—"

"Still practicing for your game show?"

I looked up, and Amanda was standing in front

of our table (we always sit in the same corner in the lunchroom, and we call it the Unicorner).

"Only a little bit," Jessica replied. "We don't need to practice very much, seeing as how we're such good friends."

"Well, I just wanted to come over and wish you luck," Amanda said.

I couldn't believe it. Amanda Harmon, wishing us luck? There had to be a catch. But she looked so sincere, I almost thought she was being honest.

"Gee, thanks," Lila said. "We really appreciate it."

"No problem," Amanda said. "I just figured, well, you're going to need some luck. Actually, you're going to need a lot of it to beat us—the Eights are going to be your opponents."

"You're what?" Mandy sputtered.

"Yeah, we faxed a letter in to Brandon Blitzen yesterday morning, and he got back to us last night," Amanda explained. "Actually, we called him. You know, it's the only way to get things done. And it turned out that they didn't have any opponents for you yet, if you can believe that."

"Actually, I can't," Mary muttered.

"Yeah, this sounds incredibly suspicious, for some reason," Evie said.

"Well, I guess they had to rearrange the schedule a little bit, because we couldn't make it the following Thursday," Amanda admitted. "So we just traded places with the boys you were originally scheduled to compete against." She shrugged. "Kind of amazing, huh? We'll all be on TV together.

Well, have a nice afternoon." She threw us a phony smile, then walked off.

Jessica's fork dropped to her plate with a loud clatter. "She's unbelievable."

"I think I just lost my appetite," Lila said, setting down her turkey sandwich. "For the next week, anyway."

"Can you believe the nerve?" Mandy practically shouted. "Just because we get on *Best Friends*, they have to, too?"

"Can't they think of one original thing to do?" Maria added. "Or do they just have to copy us in everything!"

"Come on, you guys—don't let her get to you," I said. "You're forgetting something. We're going to win, right?"

But all of a sudden, no one seemed that confident anymore.

"So I heard you guys are going to be on TV," Rick Hunter said as he passed by me and Maria. We were standing by our lockers after school on Thursday.

I nodded. "A week from today, actually."

"Cool," Rick said, nodding. "I hope you win."

"Thanks," I said. Rick is a really nice guy, most of the time.

"I heard the Eights are going up against you," Aaron Dallas said as he came up behind Rick.

"Yeah," Maria said. "We just found that out ourselves."

"It's not going to be easy to beat them, you know," Aaron commented.

"What makes you say that?" Maria asked.

"I don't know." Aaron shrugged. "They just seem like they hate to lose. Amanda's in a bunch of my classes, and it kills her if she doesn't get the best grades on tests and stuff."

"Yeah, and Julia's the same way," Rick commented. "She got an eighty-five on a quiz and she acted like the world had ended."

I slipped my backpack over my shoulder. "Well, we've been rehearsing a lot. No matter how competitive they are, I think we're going to win."

"Better than that," Maria said, nodding as she took her jacket out of her locker. "I predict we'll win *big*."

"Well, we'll be watching," Rick said. "Hey, do you think we can be in the studio audience?"

"Sure," I said. "I think they have about a hundred or so seats at the studio. You could probably call and get tickets. It's right in downtown Sweet Valley."

Rick nodded. "I'll do that."

"Well, we'd better get going," Maria said. "We have to get home and watch this week's show."

"See you guys later," I said, and we walked down the hall.

"I can't believe everyone knows all about the show already," Maria said. "It kind of makes me nervous, thinking about Aaron and Rick and half of Sweet Valley watching us."

"I know," I said as I pushed open the front door and saw the rest of the Unicorns waiting for us on the school steps.

"What took you so long?" Lila asked. "Come on, we have to hurry."

I looked at my watch. "The show's not on for another hour."

"I know, but we have to hit the mall before we watch it," Lila said.

"Why?" Maria asked.

"We have some major shopping to do," Jessica said. "Especially now that the Eights are going to be on stage with us. We *have* to look better than they do."

"But it doesn't matter what we look like, it only matters if we get the answers right," I said.

"Elizabeth." Lila shook her head. "How many times do I have to tell you—half of winning at anything is looking good."

Jessica took my arm and led me toward the bicycle rack. "We're going to intimidate them. We're going to look so confident, they won't be able to answer anything right."

"Jessica, it's not a boxing match," I said, laughing.

"No, I know. It's bigger than that," Jessica said in a serious voice as she unlocked her bicycle from the rack. "More like the Olympics."

We must have gone into every single store in the mall. Every store that sells girls' clothes, anyway.

First Jessica and Mandy thought we should all dress alike, but we couldn't agree on what to wear. Plus, the Eights always dressed the same, and we didn't want to copy them. So then Mandy decided that if we all wore something purple underneath our Unicorn jackets, it would be enough of a statement. Never mind that we all already own a ton of purple clothes: T-shirts, turtlenecks, sweaters, socks, even purple jeans. We had to get new ones, or at least think about it. Sometimes Lila forgets that we all don't have our own credit cards and fathers who'll buy us anything we want.

"How about if we all get the same earrings?" Evie suggested. "They wouldn't have to be expensive. Maybe we can find some unicorns, or else just wear plain purple studs."

"I think if we're going to wear the same earrings, they should be big," Ellen said. "Otherwise they won't show up on TV."

"Some of us don't even have pierced ears," Mary reminded everyone. "That's not going to work."

"How about if you got your ears pierced for the show?" Jessica asked.

Mary shook her head. "My mom will absolutely not let me. Anyway, it's not worth it, just for the show."

"What do you mean, *just* for the show? It's only the most important thing that's going to happen to us all year," Lila replied in an irritated tone.

"Let's think about something else, if earrings

won't work," I said, interrupting. I didn't want to have an argument over something as silly as that. "We could get matching necklaces."

"Or T-shirts, purple with white unicorns on them," Maria suggested.

"No, we're going to be wearing our new jackets, and we don't want to go too overboard," Jessica said. Tom Sanders, the man who had directed the movie that had just been filmed in town—the one Maria had been in—had given us all jackets with *Unicorns* stitched in script across the back. It was in return for helping him out with the filming. (We didn't actually film anything, but we did figure out the wardrobe for the extras in the movie—all vintage clothes, mostly put together by Mandy.)

"So if we're not going to buy anything, what are we doing here?" Ellen asked.

Mandy pointed to the large clock in the middle of the food court. "Missing *Best Friends*, that's what!"

I looked at the clock: it was quarter after four. By the time we got home, the show would be all over. "Maybe somebody taped it?" I said hopefully.

"Maybe we can watch it down at Mr. Appliance!" Jessica suggested, and the eight of us took off running down the middle of the mall. People practically jumped to get out of our way. I guess a herd of sprinting Unicorns can be pretty scary.

But when we got to Mr. Appliance, it took us a minute to find a television tuned to Channel 32, and even then, we couldn't hear the sound over the forty other TVs that were being demonstrated to other customers. I was watching *Best Friends*, but hearing an old *Beverly Hillbillies* episode.

"We missed it!" Evie said, panting from our sprint through the Valley Mall. "Now what are we going to do?"

"Maybe we could call Brandon and ask him for some sample questions," Ellen said.

"And maybe not," Lila said with a frown.

"Hey, don't worry. We've seen the show a dozen times, right?" Mandy said. "There's no way he's going to ask us something we don't know. And there's definitely no way the Eights are going to win."

"I hope he asks us what we think of our opponents," Jessica grumbled. "Because I know exactly what I'd say."

"Speaking of which, I think we should do something besides dress well to try to psych them out," Mary said. "I mean, they think they're so great now that they got on the show, like they didn't already consider themselves rulers of the planet. What if we tried to get some publicity or something, get everyone behind us before the show even starts?"

"That is a great idea," Jessica said. "You mean, like a preview on TV?"

"I doubt we could get that," Mary said. "But maybe a newspaper article or something like that."

Lila grinned and put her arm around Mary's shoulder. "How would I describe my best friends? Brilliant. Absolutely brilliant."

Five

When we got home twenty minutes later, I called Mrs. Willard at the day-care center to make sure we were still on for taking the kids to the football game on Saturday. She said that about six of the kids wanted to go, and they'd already gotten permission from their parents. I loved doing things with the kids on Saturdays, and they seemed to have a lot of fun, too.

Lila called that night to tell us she'd contacted some college friend of her father's who worked as the local editor at the *Sweet Valley Tribune.* It didn't sound as though he was too thrilled about writing an article on us, but he said he'd look into it.

"I'm sure he'll do it," Lila said. "I mean, it is one of those human-interest-type stories, and the show *is* kind of a local hit."

"Not that I don't trust Lila or anything, but what

if this guy doesn't do the article?" Jessica said after she got off the phone. "Then how can we psych out the Eights?"

"I guess we could put something about the show in the *7 & 8 Gazette*," I said. "It couldn't hurt."

"OK, but if you do, you have to make sure you quote me," Jessica said.

"I'll have to quote Amanda or someone else in her club, too," I said, "or it wouldn't be fair."

"What do you mean? You don't even have to mention them," Jessica said.

"Yes, I do," I said. "It wouldn't be good journalism to only talk about one of the clubs at school. I mean, it's pretty amazing that two clubs at our school are getting on the same show. That's news in itself."

"Can't you just slant the article, so we come off sounding better?" Jessica pleaded.

"No," I said. "Sorry."

Jessica drummed her fingers against the coffee table. "Then forget it."

"Jessica, look at it this way: it's more publicity, and there's no such thing as bad publicity, right?" That was something the adviser to the newspaper, Mr. Bowman, was always saying.

"Yes, there is," Jessica said. "When you have to share it with the Eights!"

"Check it out." Mandy handed me a can underneath the desk. "A week's worth of Medium Manly Brown."

Laughing, I turned the shiny can over in my hand. "This is really supposed to work? It looks like something I'd use on my bike." It was Friday morning, and we were in social studies class.

"I got it last night, so this morning I made an appointment for us to meet with Mr. Clark at noon," Mandy said. "We're going to do a demonstration."

"On who?" I asked.

"Well, either him, or if he doesn't want to, maybe one of those Styrofoam head models from the art studio," Mandy said. "You know, the ones we use to practice sketching facial features. You can't get much more bald than that."

I started laughing just as Jessica walked into the classroom and slammed her books on the desk next to mine. "Can you believe the utter nerve?" she muttered angrily. The final bell rang.

"Nerve of what? What's wrong?" I asked in a whisper.

"Did Mrs. Swenson make you recite poetry in front of the whole class again?" Mandy asked.

"Worse," Jessica said. "I just came from gym class. Have you guys been to the locker room yet?"

I shook my head.

"The Eights put up stickers with eight balls on them on everyone's lockers," Jessica said. "And I was late to the basketball court because I was trying to peel them all off, and I got a detention!"

Mrs. Arnette loudly cleared her throat. "What's this I hear about a detention?" She was peering at us over the top of her glasses. I realized that everyone in class had turned around and was staring at us.

"Sorry," Jessica said. "It won't happen again." She smiled her teacher smile, the one that looked very innocent, and Mrs. Arnette started class.

A minute later, Jessica handed me a note. "We have to retaliate!"

I was starting to think that Jessica would make a good army sergeant. She was sounding more and more as if she were going into battle.

Ellen tapped her foot against the carpet in the waiting room outside Mr. Clark's office. All eight of us were sitting there together, using our lunch period to show him the hair spray. "I hope he's in a good mood," Ellen said. "He's probably still mad at me."

"Don't worry, Ellen. You guys just leave it to me," Mandy said. "I've got the sales pitch down pat."

At five past noon, Mr. Clark opened the door to his office. Two parents walked out, and they didn't look very happy. "I wonder what that was all about," I whispered to Ellen.

"As long as it's not my parents in there, I don't care," she said, a worried expression on her face.

"Girls?" Mr. Clark prompted. "Would you like to come in now?"

We stood up and filed into his office. There weren't enough chairs for all of us, so some of us perched on the windowsill and some of us stood. Mandy gestured toward Mr. Clark's chair. "Please, sit down. We have something very exciting to show you."

Mr. Clark gave her a dubious look and settled into his large office chair. "May I presume this has something to do with my, uh—"

"Say no more, Mr. Clark. I have the answer to your problems right here," Mandy said cheerfully. "Now, everyone knows that a hair-loss experience can be very devastating."

Beside me, I heard Ellen stifle a laugh. Mandy sounded just like that ad in the magazine, and that cheesy videotape, and a bad self-help book, all in one.

"But there is hope," Mandy said. "Especially for men with partial heads of hair."

I was sitting beside Mr. Clark, and I couldn't help focusing on the ring of hair around his head. He seemed mildly amused, but I wasn't sure how long that would last.

Mandy put the plastic bag she'd been carrying on Mr. Clark's desk and took out one of the Styrofoam heads from art class. (I guess she figured it was easier than getting Mr. Clark to volunteer his own head for her demonstration.) She had drawn brown hair around the edge of the model head, so that it looked just like Mr. Clark's hairline, and she'd stuck some paintbrush bristles on top of the head, exactly where Mr. Clark had some random long strands of hair. It was all I could do to keep from cracking up.

"And what is that supposed to be?" Mr. Clark

asked. He didn't sound so amused anymore.

"Oh, this is just a model of what someone with hair loss might look like," Mandy said. She turned the head toward Mr. Clark, and I saw that she'd put eyeglasses on it, just like the ones Mr. Clark wore for reading his speeches at assemblies. "Just an example. Now, what I have here is a revolutionary new product. It replaces the need for toupees and hairpieces; it's less expensive; it's more convenient; it's—"

"What *is* it?" Mr. Clark demanded impatiently.

Completely unfazed by his tone, Mandy smiled and took the can of spray-on hair out of the bag. "This is a miracle hair-builder product. Watch and see how this simple spray can make it look as if this dummy has a full head of hair."

Mr. Clark didn't seem happy about the use of the word *dummy* in association with a nearly bald head. But he continued to sit there as Mandy vigorously shook the can.

"OK, now." Mandy took off the cap and started to spray Medium Manly Brown onto the Styrofoam. "See how it bonds with the hair that's already there to create the look of a full head of hair?" she asked. But as the spray settled onto the dummy's head, it didn't stick. Instead the dark brown liquid ran down the sides, making a small pool on Mr. Clark's desk.

"That's enough!" Mr. Clark cried, jumping up from his chair and sweeping the Styrofoam head off his desk into the trash can.

"Sorry." Mandy grabbed some Kleenex from the box on his desk and started to clean up the mess. "I really thought it would work, because—"

"Of course it wouldn't work," Mr. Clark said, frowning at us. "I don't know whose idea this was . . ." He stared at Mandy for a second. "But this is the stupidest, most irresponsible— I asked you to do something very simple. I only want you to replace what you destroyed. I don't want a videotape, I don't want a chintzy replacement toupee, and I definitely don't want to spray on my hair every morning! Is that so difficult to understand?"

"We're sorry," I said. I'd had no idea how much this all really upset Mr. Clark. Now I felt guilty that we'd taken it so lightly when it meant so much to him. I guess we had always thought having a toupee was kind of funny, because some of them looked so bad, but it obviously wasn't funny when *you* were the person who needed to wear one. "We're *really* sorry," I said again. "What can we do to make it up to you?"

"What I asked for in the first place," Mr. Clark replied. "I know you don't have a lot of extra money, but you're going to have to figure out a way to pay me the three hundred dollars you owe me. Middle-school principals aren't rich, you know."

"I'll have Daddy write you a check," Lila said nervously. "I can probably get it over here by the end of the day. He can send it by messenger."

Mr. Clark sat back down at his desk. "Lila, that's very generous, but it's not right. You're all in this together. You can't bail out your friends all the time. No, there's only one solution. We'll set up a payment schedule, and I'll order my new hairpiece. By the time it's ready, you'll have paid me back."

"So . . . what are you saying?" Jessica asked. "How long do we have?" She sounded like someone in an old, supersappy movie who had just found out she didn't have long to live.

Mr. Clark tapped a pencil against his desk. "I want fifty dollars by next week. And fifty the next, and so on. After six weeks this matter will be finished. We'll meet next Friday, and I expect to collect the first fifty. If you don't have it—and I don't like to threaten you girls, but I see no alternative—then perhaps I'll have to consider banning the Unicorns again. Now, if you don't mind, I'd like to get some lunch." He stood up and self-consciously touched the hair above his ears.

Mandy tossed the hair spray into his trash can on the way out of his office. "Fifty dollars by next week? I just spent seven ninety-five, plus two dollars in shipping charges, getting that stupid spray."

"How are we supposed to come up with fifty dollars?" Ellen complained as we walked toward the cafeteria. We were moving at a snail's pace, we were so depressed. "What does he expect us to do, get full-time jobs or something?" Ellen asked, with a whine in her voice.

"Yeah, maybe we should just drop out of

school," Jessica said. "I'm sure he'd love that."

"Wait a second—getting jobs isn't such a bad idea," I said.

"Elizabeth, if you want to flip burgers for the rest of your life, go ahead, but—"

"No, not that. Look, kids make money all the time by mowing lawns, baby-sitting, stuff like that," I said. "Why don't we try to do as many odd jobs as we can find? Between the eight of us, if we each get a couple of jobs in the next week, we'll easily make fifty dollars. It wouldn't be that hard, either." I'd done odd jobs before. Sometimes they turned out to be lousy, but not always.

"How are we going to find enough jobs?" Mary asked.

"We'll make up some flyers. We can put them up at the supermarkets in town, at the mall, maybe at the senior citizens' center. I bet we'll get enough jobs. But just remember, we might have to do some stuff we don't like," I told everyone as we entered the cafeteria.

"Such as?" Maria asked.

"I don't know. Cleaning, raking, waxing a car, maybe," I said with a shrug as we sat down in the Unicorner.

"Me? Work?" Lila asked. "I do *not* do windows."

"Come on, do you want Mr. Clark to ban the Unicorns again?" I argued.

"It won't be that bad," Mary told Lila. "We only have to do it long enough to pay back Mr. Clark. Then we can retire."

"I think it's a great idea," Mandy said. "We have to do something to earn the money or we'll be in even bigger trouble. Especially me. After today, I don't think Mr. Clark's going to be a fan of mine for a long time."

Ellen laughed. "The look on his face when you started spraying that stuff!"

"It looked like shoe polish," Evie said, giggling. "And I loved the way you put those bristles on top!"

"Talk about representational art," Maria said. "That Styrofoam head was the mirror image of Mr. Clark."

Mandy smiled. "Well, maybe being in the doghouse for a while *was* worth it."

Six

"Nice photo," my dad said when I came downstairs for breakfast Saturday morning. He handed me a copy of the *Tribune*. Lila's picture was on the front page of the local section next to an article entitled "Best Friends Accept TV Challenge," and the subtitle was "Local Club to Appear on Game Show."

"All right!" Jessica cried, standing right behind me. "What does it say?"

I skimmed the article. "Just that we'll be on the show, and that we think it's the start of something big." I puzzled over Lila's comment about starting something big. It wasn't as if there were a *Best Friends* championship round. We'd be on the show once, and that was it.

"She should have used a picture of all of us. But I guess this is better than nothing," Jessica commented as she sat down at the table to study the article. "At least the Eights don't have an article in here, too. This will pay them back for putting those stickers up all over the place."

"For now, anyway," I said. "I sure wouldn't put it past them to follow up our article with one of their own." Whenever we had an idea, they had the same idea about ten seconds later.

"We're driving you and some of the kids to the game today, right?" my father asked, handing me a pitcher of orange juice.

"Yeah, at about eleven, if that's OK," I said. We were meeting everyone over at the day-care center and going over in four or five cars.

"Watch the Eights show up with a bunch of kids *they're* baby-sitting," Jessica predicted.

"They won't," I said. "I think they're too selfish to care about anyone else."

"Elizabeth!" My mother sounded—and looked— shocked. "I've never heard you say something like that before, about anyone."

When it comes to judging people, I have a reputation in our house for being the nicest, and the most understanding. Which I usually am. "I guess it didn't come out right," I said. "But, Mom, you have to meet these girls. They're just—"

"Horrible," Jessica chimed in.

"They made it their goal in life to irritate us," I explained. "Whatever we do, they have to do—and do better. Like the game show. And they're so obnoxious about it."

My father shook out the newspaper section he was reading. "Just make sure you don't sink to their level. You know the only thing to do in a situation like that is to not let them get to you."

"You're right," I said. "I know. Well, today we can just have fun with Oliver, Allison, Sandy, Arthur, Ellie, and Yuky, and forget all about the Eights and the *Best Friends* show. Right, Jessica?"

She looked at me and nodded, but I could tell her mind was a million miles away. I was sure she was thinking about how she wanted to "retaliate" for the locker stickers, and what would be the best way to bug Amanda.

"I put up some flyers on the way over here," I told Ellen and Maria when I saw them at the day-care center. "I put down our phone number, because I figured it would be easier to have only one number. Then, when someone calls, I can call people and figure out who wants which job."

"I want the job where you just have to show up," Maria said.

"I want the baby-sitting assignment where I sit on the couch and watch TV, because the kids are already asleep," Ellen said. "For ten dollars an hour."

I laughed. "Come on, you guys aren't *that* lazy."

"I know. I just wish we didn't have to do it this week. I already feel insanely busy with the game show on Thursday. Plus we still have some practicing and memorizing to do," Maria said. "Because I, for one, do not plan on looking stupid on camera. I just got over a major case of stage fright, and it wasn't fun!"

Maria had had a hard time before the filming of Tom Sanders's movie because she'd lost her self-confidence and suddenly thought she couldn't act anymore. She'd become convinced that she was washed up as an actress, and it took all of us to convince her that wasn't true.

Just then, Arthur jumped out of his parents' van and came running toward us at top speed.

"Maybe we should have Arthur do our odd jobs," Maria said. "Talk about extra energy."

Allison and Sandy got dropped off a few minutes later. Allison ran right up to me and gave me a big hug.

I guess I've always wanted a little sister. Having Allie around is perfect. I can see her when I want to, but I don't have to share my room or anything like that. (By the way, Jessica and I did share a room until last year. It's a good thing we don't anymore. Not that I hated sharing, but Jessica's the most incredible slob. You can never find anything in her room, sometimes not even the bed.)

It took us about fifteen minutes to get everyone ready and to get the right number of Unicorns and kids in each car.

Sweet Valley was playing Big Mesa Middle School, one of our biggest rivals. The games between them are almost always really close, and hundreds of people show up to watch because the towns are right next to each other. That Saturday was no exception. By the time we all got ourselves and the kids organized with a buddy system and made it to the game, the bleachers were almost full.

As we got closer to the field and the bleacher area, I saw Peter Burns handing out small newspapers from a large stack piled beside him. "Peter, what's that?" I asked.

"Don't you remember? We did a special sports edition for the game today," Peter said, smiling as he handed me one of the newspapers. It was only four pages—about half the length of a normal *7 & 8 Gazette.*

"That's right," I said. I'd forgotten, because I wasn't working on the edition in any way. It's kind of weird this year, because in the sixth grade I used to be editor-in-chief of the *Sweet Valley Sixers,* and now I'm just a reporter for the *Gazette.* I only have articles in every other issue or so.

Jessica took a newspaper, too, and opened it. "I want to see if there's a picture of that gorgeous football player. I think his name is Erik— Oh, no! Don't even tell me. I don't believe this. You guys! Look at this!" She folded back the paper and pointed to a large, boxed article.

"Eights Compete on *Best Friends* Thursday," the headline read.

"Since when is being on a game show a *sport*?" Ellen wanted to know.

"How come they get an article in here and we don't?" Lila asked, turning to me.

"I don't know," I said. "I didn't hear anything about this!"

"Elizabeth, I told you we should have had an article in here," Jessica said. "I mean, they sure had the article slanted toward them! We're barely even mentioned in here."

"They must know someone on the staff," Lila said. "Someone high up."

"Look at it this way: we got in the *Tribune*," Mandy said. "And a lot more people look at that than read the *Gazette*."

"Yeah, but look." Jessica pointed to the rapidly disappearing stack of newspapers. "Everyone *we* know reads the *Gazette*. One of the Eights must have overheard us at the mall talking about having an article in the paper. So of course then they had to do the same thing. I cannot even believe them!"

"Well, there's nothing we can do about it now, and we're going to have a mutiny on our hands if we don't sit down fast," Mary said.

"There's some room over there," I said, pointing to a bleacher in front.

"We won't be able to see anything," Yuky complained.

"You're right. OK, how about up there?" I took Allison's hand and we climbed up the bleachers to about the tenth row up, with the rest of the Unicorns and kids following us. It took some doing, but we all found room for ourselves, with some of the kids sitting in our laps and some standing on the wooden bleacher so they could see.

We'd only been sitting there a minute when Arthur said, "I want some popcorn."

Oliver didn't miss a beat. "Me, too! And a soda!"

"I want a hot dog," Sandy declared. "With ketchup, relish, and mustard!"

"We have to wait until halftime," I told them.

"What's halftime?" Allison asked me.

"In about half an hour. Then we can get back down, and you can have a snack. OK? Now, let's just watch the game." I tousled Allie's hair. Then I pointed toward the field. "See the guy in the blue uniform, the one with the ball—"

Oliver stood beside Jessica, shouting at the top of his lungs: "Tackle him! Get him! Clobber him!"

Jessica tapped him on the shoulder. "I don't want to go deaf, you know. Maybe you could yell a little less loudly?"

"Sure!" Oliver grinned, turned back to the game, and screamed, "Get that guy! Tackle him! What are you waiting for?" Jessica tapped him again, and he turned to her. "You said a little," Oliver said, smiling.

We were all standing around the concession stands, which are right by the bleachers, at halftime, getting the kids some snacks. Half of us were watching the kids, while the other half stood in line to get food. I was one of the ones watching the kids. Jessica was in line with my ten-dollar bill. I kind of doubted that I would see any change.

About five minutes into halftime, I saw the

Eights coming down from the bleachers, headed for where we were standing.

Mandy spotted them, too. "Give me a break," she said. "Are they all wearing the same outfit, or am I seeing things?"

"It's like camp—they must have a list of all the clothes they have to have," Ellen said.

"I am so glad we only wear the same color," Evie said. "They look ridiculous."

The Eights were all wearing blue Sweet Valley Middle School sweatshirts, khaki shorts, and white tennis sneakers. When they got closer, I saw they all had on white socks with tiny black eight balls on them.

"Maybe they look silly, but they *do* look like a team," Lila observed. "I wonder what they're up to now."

I was so busy staring at Amanda and her friends and thinking about how they'd slipped that article into the paper, that for a minute I forgot we were supposed to be watching the kids. When I looked around, I saw them all playing catch with a small red plastic football just off to one side of the bleachers. "Come on, you guys. Forget about the Eights. We have six kids to watch!"

I hurried over to make sure all the kids were still there. Lila and I quickly took a head count: "Arthur, Oliver, Sandy, Ellie . . ."

"That's only four," I said. "Where are Allison and Yuky?" I looked in every direction, standing on my tiptoes. So did Lila, while Mandy, Ellen, and

Evie kept track of the kids who were playing football.

"Who here was Allison's buddy?" Lila asked me.

"Yuky," I said with a sigh.

"Uh-oh. Maybe we'd better ask the announcer to say something," Lila said. "We could ask him to have the kids meet us right there, by the hot dog booth."

"OK," I said. "You do that, and I'll start searching. Mandy, go wait by the hot dog booth in case they hear the announcement and show up there."

I started hunting all around the bleachers, trying to figure out where Yuky and Allison would go. They might have wanted to play on the soccer field, so I ran over and checked there. Then I looked at the cotton candy booth, since I knew Allison loved sweets. I thought I saw her for a second, but when I got closer, it turned out to be another little girl.

I made a huge circle around the field, calling Allison's and Yuky's names and asking people if they'd seen two small girls go past. After a couple of minutes, I started getting really worried. What if they were feeling hopelessly lost, like we'd abandoned them? What if something had happened to them? "Allison! Yuky!" I called. It was my responsibility to look out for them, and it was all my fault they were gone.

I had almost finished making a complete circle of the football field when I saw what looked like a small Korean-American girl. I hurried closer, straining my eyes. It was Yuky! She was talking to a boy who looked a lot like her—only several feet taller.

"Elizabeth! This is my cousin!" Yuky yelled to me. "Come here and meet him!"

I walked over to them. "Yuky, you shouldn't just run off like that," I said. "We were worried about you!"

"I'm sorry," Yuky said. "This is my cousin Joe."

"Hi," I said, looking around for Allison.

"Nice to meet you. Actually, it's my fault," Joe said. "I was just getting some lemonade when I saw Yuky. I kept asking her if she should tell someone where she was going, but she said no. I didn't really believe her."

"That's OK. Where's Allison, Yuky?" I asked.

"Here I am!" Allison came running out from behind one of the football teams' benches. "I win at hide-and-seek!"

"Allie, it's not a good time to play hide-and-seek, OK?" I said, giving her a quick hug. I felt so relieved, it was almost like my legs were going to collapse underneath me. "We thought you were lost."

"I'm really sorry," Joe said again.

"It's OK—as long as they're both all right. You have a very cute cousin here, but she does get into trouble." I smiled and ruffled Yuky's black hair with my hand. "Hey, we should get back to our seats before the second half starts. Besides, I want to tell everyone that I found you."

"Were they worried?" Allison asked.

"Of course!" I told her. "Me most of all. But don't worry, I'm sure someone saved you a hot dog." We got back to the rest of the group just as the announcer asked for Yuky and Allison to report to the concession stand area. *Oh, great!* I thought. *Now the Eights, and everyone else, will know the Unicorns can't even keep track of six little kids.*

"Here we are!" Allison jumped up and down.

I looked at Mandy and let out a deep breath. "That was a close one."

"I'm so glad you guys are OK," she said, hugging both of them. "Hey, Elizabeth, maybe we should have the announcer advertise our new odd-jobs service. I bet we'd get lots of customers."

Lila groaned as we made our way back to the bleachers. "I am not doing anyone's laundry or scrubbing any floors or—"

"Let's just make this short. What *will* you do?" Mandy teased her.

"Phone calls," Lila said. "I'm good at those. Or else I could be someone's personal shopper for a day."

"They'd probably go broke," I said.

We got settled back in our seats, and I thought the game was about to start up again, when the announcer said, "And now, ladies and gentlemen, for an end-of-halftime treat . . . here comes the Eight Times Eight Club, with a new cheer they've written just for today's game!"

We all turned to each other. Jessica's cup dropped down onto the ground. Lila looked as if she had seen a ghost. Ellen was picking popcorn out of the bag to eat, and she kept missing her mouth, as if she were asleep.

"Tell me this is a bad dream," Maria said, craning her neck to get a view of the field as some bouncy dance music blasted through the speakers.

"It's a nightmare, and it's happening to us," Lila said.

The Eights bounded onto the field in their identical outfits, with Amanda at the front of the formation, of course.

"Like they even know the first thing about leading a cheer," Jessica grumbled. She was a member of the Boosters last year, and she takes cheerleading pretty seriously. "Who do they think they are?"

The Eights went through a series of dance moves to the music—all perfectly synchronized. They looked pretty good, considering they'd probably only put the cheer together that week.

"I wonder what gave them the idea to do this," Mary said to me. "I mean, *we* didn't do a cheer."

The music suddenly stopped and the Eights stood, facing the home crowd. "Sweet Valley, Sweet Valley, we're number one," they chanted. "We know how to win, and we'll get the job done."

Jessica turned to me and rolled her eyes. "How original."

Still, when the Eights were finished with their cheer and finished with another sequence of dance moves, the crowd erupted into such applause, you'd think they'd just put on a Grammy-winning performance. People around us were even standing and cheering for them. "Let's hear it for the Eight Times Eight Club!" the announcer cried.

"Rah rah," Lila muttered.

"Wasn't that fantastic?" I heard an older girl sitting next to us ask the boy next to her.

"They're great dancers," he agreed. "And they're so cute!"

None of us could say anything, we were so demoralized. But I knew what we were all thinking.

1. We could have done better than that.
2. Why didn't we think of that?
3. The Eights are even one *more* up on us now.
4. We've got to beat them on *Best Friends*, no matter what.

Seven

On Sunday morning, I posted more flyers advertising the Unicorn Club's new odd-jobs service. Then I tried to catch up on my homework—I knew we'd be busy cramming for *Best Friends* during the rest of the week. Everyone had been even more determined to win since the Eights had done their little cheer on Saturday, not to mention their huge "ad" in the school paper. Jessica was so depressed about it, she kept wandering around the house on Sunday, muttering. "I can't get that stupid cheer out of my head. Sweet Valley, Sweet Valley, we're number one," she'd mumble as she went by me. "Crazy Eights, Crazy Eights, you're not so great," she'd say. "I'd like to hit you with a dinner plate."

"Hey, Jessica, chill out!" I told her when she walked in front of me for the hundredth time. I was sitting on the couch trying to read a book for

English class. "If you think about it too much, you won't do well on the show."

Jessica glared at me. "Oh, so now you're for the Eights, too?"

"What? What are you talking about? All I meant was, don't go crazy over this. It's not worth it. If we win, great. If we don't, it's not the end of the world." I picked up my book and started reading again.

Jessica peered over the top of my book. "Excuse me? Did you just say that it wouldn't be the end of the world if we lost?"

"Well, you know what I meant," I said. "Of course we're going to win. For one thing, we're a lot smarter than they are, and for another, we've practiced so much, I could recite everyone's personal history if I had to."

"Which we *will* have to," Jessica said. "Don't forget that."

Just then the telephone rang. Jessica ran into the kitchen so she could grab it before Steven did. Half the time, he tells our friends we're not home just because he's too lazy to run downstairs to get us.

"Hello?" I heard Jessica say. "Um, that's right, this is the Unicorns Odds and Ends Service. Uh-huh. Right. Sure, someone could do that for you. What time? OK. Fine. Thanks a lot!"

She came back into the living room with a big grin on her face. "I got a job for you."

"Really? Wait a second. What do you mean, *you* got it? I'm the one who put up all the signs."

"Do you want to pay back Mr. Clark or don't you?" Jessica replied. "Anyway, this job sounds perfect for you. It's housecleaning, and they're going to pay five dollars an hour for two hours."

"When do they want someone?" I asked, wondering how come *I* was perfect for that job. It seemed as if anyone could do it, including Jessica. We were supposed to be in this together.

"This afternoon. This woman's having a party tonight, and she needs help getting her house ready. Here's the address." Jessica handed me a piece of paper.

So much for getting ahead on my homework. "OK, but if other people call while I'm gone, you have to coordinate this whole thing and call people to do the jobs."

"No problem," Jessica said. "That will be *my* job: employment coordinator."

I shook my head and stood up. Trust Jessica to get out of doing any *real* work.

We got more phone calls for odd jobs later that day and on Monday, and everyone spent part of Tuesday afternoon after school working—some people for just half an hour, some for three or four. We were so busy between school, extracurricular stuff, and working, it was hard to remember that we were supposed to be practicing. We were going to be on television in only two days! But we each made up some study sheets on ourselves for everyone to review while they were out walking dogs or sweeping the sidewalks or scrubbing bathtubs (I kind of felt sorry for Ellen, who got stuck cleaning a house that sounded as though it hadn't been touched in a year).

I wasn't worried about the show. Doing all that work kind of took our minds off the Eights and how competitive this whole thing had gotten, between the newspaper articles, the stickers, and everything else.

On Wednesday morning we went into school early to hang banners we'd made the night before to advertise our TV appearance. We thought we'd had a completely original idea, but as usual, it turned out the Eights were there, too. I don't even think anyone was surprised at that point. It was almost as if they had a spy working for them, someone following us and listening to our every conversation.

"As if getting up early wasn't bad enough," Jessica grumbled.

"What are you doing here?" Amanda asked.

"Just hanging some banners," Lila said. "Not that it's any business of yours."

Amanda stared at the banner Maria and Evie were holding between them. It said: T.V. HISTORY WILL BE MADE TOMORROW! CHEER THE UNICORNS TO VICTORY! "None of our business, huh?" she asked, raising one eyebrow.

"Hold your end up a little higher," Jessica told Mary, completely ignoring Amanda. Mary was standing on the stairs, hanging the other banner we'd made. In bright purple paint, it said: WATCH THE UNICORNS TRAMPLE THE "CRAZY" EIGHTS.

Julia started smoothing out the banner she and Marcy were carrying, spreading it out onto the floor. THE EIGHTS ON TV! TUNE IN AND SEE WHO'S *RE- ALLY* BEST FRIENDS.

"Yeah, right," Mandy muttered. "As if anyone could beat us."

"We're so ready, it's ridiculous," Lila said. "I mean, I know so much about everyone, I could write a book."

Amanda folded her arms across her chest. "Why don't you, then?"

"Maybe I will," Lila replied calmly. "But in the meantime, I'm going to look forward to seeing your face when we win tomorrow."

"What makes you so sure you're going to?" Julia asked, taping their banner on the other side of the hall, opposite ours. "I can just tell. For one thing, Jessica and I have been best friends for over a decade," Lila said. I had to laugh when she said the word *decade*. "I know more about her than Elizabeth does, even. And for another, we've been practicing for a week and a half, unlike some people who found out they were going to be on the show less than a week ago."

"We don't need as much time," Marcy said, pulling a long piece of masking tape off the roll.

"Anyway, aren't you guys too busy washing windows and mowing lawns to be on the show to-morrow?" Amanda asked. "It's OK, we'll tell

Brandon you needed to forfeit. He'll understand."

Mandy shook her head. "Not a chance. You're not going to get out of it that easily."

"Who's trying to get out of it?" Amanda asked in an innocent voice. "All I was saying was, I know you guys are so broke and everything. Why else would you be volunteering to walk people's St. Bernards and—"

"That's our business and no one else's," Jessica said in a haughty tone.

"Really? It wouldn't have anything to do with Mr. Clark's toupee, would it?" Marcy asked. Everyone at school knew about Jessica swiping Mr. Clark's toupee. But what did that have to do with the game show?

"I thought we were talking about the *Best Friends* show," Mandy said. "What do you care if we work or don't work?"

"Oh, I don't," Amanda said innocently. "I just wanted to let you know, if you *want* to drop out, there's still time. We really won't think any less of you."

"Drop out? Of *Best Friends?*" I asked her. Even I was getting angry now. "I don't think so. It was our idea to be on the show in the first place."

"Yeah, and it was Elizabeth's letter that helped us become contestants," Evie said, walking toward Amanda. I'd never seen her look so irritated before. "There's no way we're going to not show up. What are you, scared to face us?"

"Of course, if you *are* scared, you can stay home

tomorrow afternoon instead of going to the studio," Lila added. "We'll play just to see how many points we get."

"At least a couple hundred," Jessica said. The top scores were usually around eighty or ninety.

"Yeah, right," Julia said.

"As if," Marcy added.

"There's no way you're going to get more points than we are," Amanda confidently declared.

"Oh, really?" Jessica gave her a critical look. "Want to bet?"

Uh-oh, I said to myself. *Not another one of Jessica's bets.* She's made so many bets—and *lost* so many bets—over the years, that I can't even keep track of them anymore. She and Steven make bets almost every other week. I hope she never goes to Las Vegas or she'll be in big trouble.

"Sure," Amanda said with a shrug. "I love making bets I know I'm going to win. What's the bet?"

"Let me think . . ." Jessica stared at the ceiling.

"Shouldn't we have some say in what the bet is?" Julia asked.

"No. We made the challenge, so we get to choose the bet," Lila said. "This might take a minute. Come on, everyone." She gestured for all of us to come over by the stairwell, where we gathered in a huddle.

"What are we going to make them do?" Ellen asked.

"Something that would be really humiliating," Lila said.

"If they lose tomorrow, that's going to be humiliating enough, isn't it?" I asked.

"Elizabeth, that's not the point, as Mr. Clark would say," Mandy told me. "If by some fluke they won, do you know how miserable they'd make *us*? You know what they're like. Anyway, it doesn't have to be so horrible."

"Yeah, it can just be something they'd hate to do," Evie said.

"We could make them all wear different clothes for once," Maria joked.

Mandy laughed. "That would be horrible, for them. How about something embarrassing they'd have to do, here at school?"

"That reminds me." Jessica looked at Mandy. "Remember that time when you made me sing in the lunchroom last year? When we had master-servant day?" Mandy nodded. "*That* was pretty humiliating."

"Yeah, people were coming up to you and imitating you for weeks after that," I said. Jessica had had to sing "Feelings" in front of the entire lunchroom, because Mandy was angry at her for something Jessica had made *her* do earlier. "How about if we make the bet that the losers have to perform in the cafeteria?"

"OK, but *what* do they have to perform?" Mary asked.

"Let's think of the worst, most childish, or most obnoxious song there is," Ellen said. "How about something like . . . what's it called, it's one of my mom's favorite sóngs and it's really— Oh, 'I Am Woman'! Do you guys know that one?"

"Yeah, but I think we need something even dippier," Jessica said. "I know, how about if we make them sing a *disco* song. You know, like from those old movies where everyone wears polyester shirts and tight bell-bottom jeans, and they look completely stupid."

"Not bad," Mandy said. "But I think they might pull that off somehow, like they did with that cheer. Besides, that stuff is kind of hip again. How about this: They're really into being eighth graders, right? So let's make them do something that's incredibly babyish."

I don't know how the idea came into my head. I wasn't even really trying to think hard about what song to pick. But all of a sudden I just said, " 'Puff the Magic Dragon.' "

A grin spread across Jessica's face. Lila smiled, too, and then Mandy put her arm around my shoulders. "Excellent. We can even make them dress up in costumes if we want."

"OK!" Jessica strolled back over to Amanda, who had just finished hanging the banner so that it was the first thing kids would see when they walked into school. "Here's the deal. Whoever loses . . ." She paused and glanced at each of us and smiled, as if to say, *And we know who* that *will be.* "Has to get up in the cafeteria the day after the show and sing 'Puff the Magic Dragon' in front of everybody. No excuses."

"No excuses? Are you sure about that?" Amanda asked. It sounded like a challenge.

"Yeah, you wouldn't want to get into something you couldn't get out of," Julia added.

"Oh, we're not worried." Mandy grinned.

"OK, you guys, I know everyone's tired, but this is serious," Mandy said that evening. We'd all gone to Casey's after dinner for a last-minute study session, since on Thursday we'd have to go straight from school to the studio.

I was surprised our parents let me and Jessica go out on a school night, but I think they were as anxious to see us win as we were to win. Even Steven seemed a little excited about our being on the show. (But in exchange for his coming to the studio and cheering, we had to promise we'd spend some of our gift certificates on him.)

"I can't believe I spent the whole afternoon pulling weeds out of Mrs. Manning's garden," Lila grumbled. "My back is killing me."

"Yeah, well, at least you didn't have to chase triplets around all afternoon," Mary said. "It was fun at first, but by the time their parents got home, I must have run about five miles, just around the house." She put a big spoonful of chocolate frozen yogurt into her mouth.

"So what's left to practice?" I asked. I took a bite of my strawberry sundae. I was starving, even though we'd just had dinner, because I'd spent all afternoon cleaning out our neighbors' garage.

There must have been about thirty boxes of junk they didn't use anymore that needed to be dropped off at Goodwill. But they had paid me ten dollars for helping. When we combined the money we'd all made so far, we had forty-five dollars—almost enough to give Mr. Clark his first payment. I wasn't exactly looking forward to having to do the extra work for the next six weeks, but he was right, it was our responsibility to pay him back. I still couldn't get out of my head the image of his disappointed face when he saw we were giving him spray-paint hair instead of a new toupee.

"I don't know," Evie said. "I feel pretty good about this. I think I know everything I need to."

"When did Mary break her arm?" Jessica asked, licking hot fudge off her spoon.

"Fifth grade. Playing kickball," Evie said, without missing a beat.

"What's my favorite song?" Lila asked.

"'Puff the Magic Dragon,'" Evie said. "Just kidding. No, it's 'You're the One for Me,' by Johnny Buck."

"Right." Lila nodded.

"Now let me ask some questions," Evie said. "How long have I been playing the violin?"

"That's easy," Maria said. "Eight years."

Evie nodded. "OK . . . and when did my great-grandparents come to America?"

"Fifty-two years ago?" Ellen answered.

"Exactly!" Evie said excitedly. "This is great. We're so ready, they're going to have to drag us off the stage when the show's over. We're going to be like, 'Keep asking us questions! We know more than that!'"

Everyone laughed. If Evie knew about us, and even ditsy Ellen knew one of the hardest questions, I thought we'd be impossible to beat. I figured the only thing to worry about was if one of us got stage fright or froze up when the TV cameras were pointed at us.

I couldn't wait to show the Eights that we really knew what being best friends was all about. And if in the meantime we showed them we were the better club, that was just going to be icing on the cake.

Especially when they sang "Puff the Magic Dragon" in front of the entire school.

Eight

I could hardly eat anything for breakfast on Thursday. My mother made a special coffee cake with "Good Luck" written on top in icing, and I think Steven ate at least two-thirds of it. Jessica was nervous, too. She kept nibbling coffee cake, then running back upstairs to change her outfit, because we wouldn't have time to change between school and the show and she wanted it to be perfect. Finally she settled on a purple mock turtleneck, a longish black skirt, and purple-and-black-checked socks. I was wearing a lavender-colored sundress, so our purples wouldn't clash if we stood next to each other, and my favorite dressy tan sandals.

I couldn't concentrate during my classes, either. I was lucky I didn't have any tests or quizzes. During social studies class, Jessica passed me a piece of paper with a small picture of a dragon

drawn on it and the word "Puff!" I don't think any
of us ate any lunch. From time to time, we'd look
over at the Eights' table or they'd glance at us, but
we didn't say anything. I had this nervous but excited feeling in the pit of my stomach. It seemed to
be saying, *It's now or never.*

My father picked some of us up outside school
to drive over to the Vista Vision studio, and Mrs.
Riteman drove another carful. (My mother was
going to come straight from work and meet us
there. Steven and his buddies from high school
were riding their bikes.) We couldn't stop talking in
the car about what we were going to say to
Brandon, whether we should wear our Unicorn
jackets on stage at the beginning or save them until
the end when we won, and we were still discussing
who should be on which team of four.

"It doesn't matter who we want to have teamed
together," I tried telling Jessica for the tenth time as
she outlined our strategy. "Brandon draws our
names out of that big top hat, remember?"

"But maybe we could talk him into pulling out
the four names we want," Jessica said.

"Don't count on it." From what I'd seen of
Brandon Blitzen, he didn't strike me as the kind of
guy who'd listen to *us*. I mean, he was the one with
the hit show.

We parked in the lot outside the studio and went
inside. At the front desk, a woman stopped us. "May
I help you?" she asked, looking up from an appointment book. On her desk was a huge pink sign that

said VISTA VISION—THE FUTURE OF AMERICAN TV.

"Hello. We're here for *Best Friends*," Jessica said proudly.

"Studio audience?" the receptionist asked.

Jessica looked highly insulted. "Contestants!" she said.

"Oh, I'm sorry." The receptionist smiled. "Go down that hallway and take a right. That's the backstage area, and there'll be makeup people waiting for you."

"Makeup?" Jessica squeezed my arm as we walked down the hall. "We actually get our own makeup artists? See, Elizabeth? I told you we were going to become stars."

"This *is* pretty exciting," I admitted. We opened the door to the backstage area.

Inside, in a small sort of closet off to the right, one woman was standing, holding a hairbrush. There was a plain wooden chair and a small mirror on the wall in front of it.

"This *is* Channel Thirty-two," Lila said with a sigh. "Not exactly the big time, is it?" She flipped her hair over her shoulder. "I think I'll do my own hair."

"Oh, you found some spare time to come to the game after all?" Julia asked, coming out from behind one of the standing room dividers. She was wearing a white, extra-large T-shirt with a large eight ball on both the front and the back.

"Very funny," Jessica said. "So where's everyone else? Where's the audience, and where's Brandon?"

"He's talking to Amanda, over there." Julia gestured to the stage behind her. "If you go back there, you'll see everything. It's kind of a cool set, actually, even if it is budget-o-rama." She half-smiled at me, and I almost fell over. It was the first time she'd ever been sort of nice to me. I decided she must be nervous, like the rest of us.

I followed Jessica and Lila over to the stage, which was behind some more partitions. As we got closer, I could hear rumblings of people sitting down, talking, and laughing. When we came out from behind the last partition, I heard Steven yell, "All right, Jessica and Elizabeth!"

Amanda gave us one of her famous superior looks. "So you have at least one fan."

Then some of our other friends from school started cheering for the Unicorns, and I thought I heard my mom and dad chime in, too. Amanda didn't look so happy, until the other half of the audience started chanting, "Eight Times Eight, Eight Times Eight!" It was kind of amazing, considering the show hadn't even begun yet.

"So *you're* Elizabeth Wakefield." A man holding a clipboard stopped in front of me, holding out his hand for me to shake. "Dan Peterson, the contact man here at Vista Vision."

"Hi. It's nice to meet you," I said.

"It looks as if your whole team's here," Dan said. "You'll be standing over there." He pointed to the right side of the stage. "The Eights will be over there, and Brandon will be in the middle."

"Where is he, anyway?" I asked.

"He just left. He won't come back out until the show actually starts," Dan said. "We like to get the audience revved up. Helps ratings. You understand." He winked at me.

"Right," I said. Back when I had first spoken to him over the phone, I had already decided Dan had a lock on the award for Most Insincere, but today he was outdoing even himself.

"Isn't this great?" Mandy pointed to the huge, glitzy sign above the podium where Brandon would stand. It said BEST FRIENDS in large, swirling letters. "I forgot this was such a seventies-type set. We should have worn platforms or something."

I laughed. *"You* could have, anyway!"

"Look at them." Jessica gestured with her head toward the Eights, who were standing and talking to people in the front row of the audience. "They're working the crowd."

"Nice identical T-shirts," Ellen said. "I'm *so* surprised."

"Even people in the audience are wearing them." Evie pointed to a row of Eight Times Eight fans, who looked as though they must be the Eights' parents. Behind them, Steven and his friends were sitting, laughing and joking around.

"I'm glad we decided to wear our Unicorn jackets, after all," Jessica said. "They're so much cooler than those ugly T-shirts."

"OK, everyone." Dan clapped his hands together. "We're on the air in two minutes, so listen up. When I introduce you to the audience, you come running out and take your positions behind your counters here." He pointed to the long counters on each side of the stage. "And remember what I told you on the phone—you are absolutely not allowed to use any words that wouldn't get past the censors, and I'm sure you know which ones I mean. Also, remember to look at the camera sometimes, and smile a lot. Please don't talk among yourselves between questions—it's too distracting. Got all that?"

We nodded. "No problem," Jessica said.

"Now, for maybe the most important stage direction of all," Dan said. "You've got to look peppy! I want to see excited contestants out there! Now, can I see some enthusiasm?"

Amanda and the Eights immediately broke into a cheer for themselves. "Eight Times Eight, Eight Times Eight, we're the club that's really great!"

Jessica rolled her eyes. "Oh, brother. I hope they're not going to do those stupid cheers all year." Then, before I knew what she was doing, she started leading a Unicorn cheer, one she improvised on the spot. "What's the number-one club to ever be born? Unicorn, Unicorn, Unic—!"

A loud buzzer sounded, interrupting her. "Backstage, everyone!" Dan cried, shooing us off the stage.

We went back and stood in a group, and so did the Eights. We were in two huddles, like football teams before a big play. A minute later, the theme to *Best Friends* started playing, and the audience broke into applause. Evie grabbed my arm. "I'm so nervous!"

"You're going to do great," I assured her. "We all are."

"Just remember, everyone," Lila said. "We have to win, or we'll be singing 'Puff the Magic Dragon' tomorrow."

"Not to mention living in total embarrassment," Ellen added.

"What are you guys talking about? Like we're going to do anything *but* win!" Mandy exclaimed.

"And now, from Sweet Valley Middle School," Dan announced from just offstage. "Here's a group of eighth graders, please welcome . . . the Eight Times Eight Club!"

The Eights ran out onto the stage, cheering and pumping their fists in the air. I watched through a crack in one of the partitions as they took their spots behind the counter.

"And from the same school, a group of girls who claim that they're best friends, let's have a big hand for . . . the Unicorns!" Dan yelled.

"All right, Unicorns!" Mandy cried, and we ran out to take our places. The audience was making a lot of noise. I could tell each side had about the same number of fans, because for every "Go, Unicorns!" there was a "Go, Eights!" yell in reply.

I was thinking about what Dan had said when he introduced us. What did he mean, "*claimed* to be best friends"? We *were* best friends. Why did he have to say it that way? He hadn't said anything like that about the Eights.

"Ladies and gentlemen, the moment you've been waiting all week for. Presenting, the one, the only, the original, the master of MCs—"

"He's not that great," Jessica muttered to me under her breath.

"Mr. Bran . . . don . . . Blit . . . zen!" Dan cried.

Brandon Blitzen strolled out onto stage, acting as if he were one of the biggest stars in Hollywood. I guess attitude is everything, though. And he did have kind of a suave look going for him. He was wearing a navy double-breasted suit, and his blond hair was, as usual, styled perfectly, without one hair out of place. I wasn't sure, but I thought he had eye makeup on.

"Greetings," Brandon said. "Welcome to another edition of *Best Friends*, the game show that asks the question: How well do you know your best friends?" In sort of a confidential tone he added, "And sometimes makes best friends into worst enemies!"

The audience cheered loudly. I glanced across the stage at Amanda. She was grinning confidently, as if he'd just announced that her team had already won. *We'll see*, I thought. *We'll just see who the better friends are.* I was kind of surprised by my reaction. As I said before, I don't usually get very competitive. But something about being on TV, and playing against Amanda, seemed to bring it out in me.

"And now it's time to meet our teams," Brandon said. He walked over to the Eights' counter. They were lined up in a row, all wearing their eight-ball shirts. "This is the Eight Times Eight Club, and I'm wondering why they don't just call themselves the Sixty-fours." The audience laughed, and so did we.

"Good one," Mary said, nodding.

"Even Brandon Blitzen sees right through them," Lila scoffed.

"Which one of you is Amanda?" Brandon asked.

Amanda raised her hand, then spoke into the microphone. "I am. Hi, Brandon, it's so great to be here, I can't tell you."

"No, you can't, because it's my show, and I already know how great it is, don't I?" Brandon smiled, and some people in the audience laughed. I didn't think it was that funny, even if Amanda had sounded obnoxious. "I understand you're the president of this group?" Amanda nodded. "Why don't you introduce your friends, then," Brandon said.

Amanda went down the line of Eights standing behind the counter. As she did, the camera was focusing on them, and I saw Brandon take some index cards out of his pocket to look at. He wasn't paying much attention to her at all.

"All right, then." Brandon smiled. "And now, let's have a big hand for the . . ." I couldn't tell whether he'd forgotten our club name or whether he was just pausing for dramatic effect.

"The Unicorns!" Lila said enthusiastically into the microphone in front of her.

Brandon turned to her. "And you must be the club president?"

Lila shook her head. "No, actually, that's Mandy Miller." She pointed to Mandy. "I'm Lila Fowler."

"Nice to meet you, Lila. After the way you took charge just now, you must have some position of power in the Unicorns. Are you vice-president, then?" Brandon asked.

"No, she just likes to tell people what to do," Mandy joked. "But we love her anyway." People in the audience laughed.

Lila pretended to be angry for a second, and then she smiled. "What can I say? I'm a natural for president someday."

Brandon smiled. "OK, Mandy, before Lila takes over the show, why don't you introduce the rest of your club? Whoa . . . wait a second, am I seeing double?" He looked at me, then at Jessica, then at me again.

I hate when people do that.

"The one with her hair pulled back is Elizabeth Wakefield, and the one wearing her hair down is Jessica Wakefield," Mandy explained. "That's how we always tell them apart. Or, today, Elizabeth's the one with lavender dress, and Jessica's wearing purple."

I thought I heard Steven shout something, but I was pretty sure the microphones over by the studio audience didn't pick it up.

"No problem." Brandon winked at me. "And who else is in the Unicorn Club?"

Mandy went down the row, listing us in order. "Maria Slater, Evie Kim, Ellen Riteman, Mary

Wallace, me, Lila, Elizabeth, and Jessica."

"OK, then. It's time to divide our teams!" Brandon said, paying as much attention to our names as he had to the Eights'. "As you know, we have a very scientific method for this." He walked back to his podium and pulled a hat out from underneath it. "First I'll drop in the names of the Eights." He pulled slips of paper out of his left suit jacket pocket and dropped them into the hat. "Our first team to be out on stage—which means the rest of you will go backstage to our soundproof room—will be . . ." He picked out four slips, one at a time. "Julia . . . Marcy . . . Amanda . . . and . . . Carmen!"

The Eights gave each other high-fives and separated into two groups.

"For the Unicorns, we'll have . . ." Brandon pulled slips out of his right suit jacket pocket and put them into the hat. "Elizabeth . . . Lila . . . Mandy . . . and Maria!" he announced.

Mandy shouted, "Go, Unicorns!" and we all gathered in a group hug.

"Remember, we know everything, so just don't panic and we'll do fine," Lila told everyone.

"Ready, teams?" Brandon asked.

We separated and faced him again.

"It's that time. Can you prove that you're really . . . best friends?" Brandon winked at the camera, and the theme music kicked in again, as the station went to its first commercial break.

"Here goes everything," Jessica said, just before she followed Dan backstage to the soundproof room.

Nine

"Welcome back to *Best Friends*!" Brandon grinned, his teeth sparkling in the bright stage lights. "Is everybody ready?" He looked at both teams.

"Sure thing," Mandy said confidently. "Fire away."

"We're ready," Amanda said. "Go ahead. Ask us anything."

"OK. I love your enthusiasm. We'll begin with a question for Elizabeth." Brandon picked up one of the index cards from his podium. "Remember, each correct answer earns your team *ten* points. OK, here goes: What is Jessica's definition of happiness?"

"No fair," Julia complained from the other side. "They're twins."

"Maybe so, but they're on the same team," Lila said. "That's all that counts."

"Lila is correct. The questions are completely

random, anyway, so there's no way of controlling who gets asked what. Go ahead, Elizabeth."

I thought for a second. "Jessica would define happiness as an all-expenses-paid shopping spree in Beverly Hills," I said. "Wait—*if* she got to go with Johnny Buck."

"OK. The judges have recorded your answer. Now. Julia. If Gretchen could go anyplace in the world, where would it be?" Brandon asked, shuffling index cards on his desk.

"That's easy. The Mall of America," Julia said. "It's all she ever talks about."

The Mall of America? I wanted to say. *She could go anywhere in the world and she'd go to a* mall? I'd pick Paris or Switzerland or Alaska—somewhere completely new.

"Moving on, our next question is for Lila. If Ellen were sent to a desert island and could only bring one thing with her, what would it be?"

Lila smiled. "Her portable CD player. Definitely. She can't live without music. She plays the same CDs all the time and—"

"That's enough information," Brandon interrupted her. "OK, Marcy. What is Susan's idea of the perfect date? Just a brief description, please. What would be the defining characteristic?"

"The guy has to play basketball," Marcy declared. "If he doesn't, she is not interested."

"Mandy, I've got the same question for you," Brandon began, smiling at her.

"Well, I like boys who—"

"The question is about Mary," Brandon continued. "Wait until you hear the complete question, please."

"Sorry, just a little joke," Mandy said. "Mary's idea of a perfect date? He has to be preppie, like her."

"Carmen, you're up next. What is Kristin's *most* prized possession?"

Carmen snapped her gum. "I think it's her autographed picture of Brad Marshall—you know, that teen actor?"

We knew. Maria had acted in a scene with him a only few weeks ago, in the movie Tom Sanders made. We were *only* wearing jackets Tom had given us, and Maria had *only* kissed Brad in her scene.

"And Maria? What would Evie say is her most prized possession?" Brandon asked.

I wished he would vary the questions a little. I'd never realized before how boring they were.

Maria considered it for a minute. "This is a tough call. She loves to watch old movies, so I was going to say her VCR. But she also loves to play the violin, and she has been doing that for eight years—so I guess I'll go with her violin."

"Now, finally, to complete our first round: Amanda, if Erica were going on a trip and she could only bring one piece of luggage, how big would it be?"

"It definitely wouldn't be a suitcase," Amanda said, laughing. "I'll say a huge trunk."

"Good job, everyone." Brandon tapped the index cards against the podium. "When we come back, we'll find out how their team members answered the questions!"

"How do you think we did?" I asked Mandy once the cameras were off.

"Piece of cake," Mandy said. "Their answers were so dumb, there's no way someone could come up with the same ones."

"I think we did great," Lila said. "Just as we predicted."

A few minutes later, the theme music played again, and Brandon announced that the other halves of the teams were coming back "from their intense-isolation booths."

I smiled when I saw Jessica coming out onto the stage. I was so sure she was going to match my answer. I started thinking about how if we got forty points in the first round, we could miss a question in the second round and probably still come out on top. I glanced at my watch. It was quarter past four. The show was half over already!

"OK, then. Let's see how you did!" Brandon said as Dan handed him a computer printout sheet. "I have the questions and the original answers here, and we'll see if we have any matches." He smiled at us. "Do you feel lucky?"

We all nodded. "I know I do," Ellen said.

"Besides, it's not about luck," Lila said breezily. "It's about how well we know each other, like you said."

"True," Brandon said, nodding. "Too true. So let's see. Jessica, you're first in line here. What is your definition of happiness? We've heard what Elizabeth had to say, now let's hear your answer."

"My definition of happiness . . ." Jessica rested her elbow on the counter and stared into space for a second. "Well, I guess I'd have to say that it would be having my family safe and happy. If they're happy, then I am, too."

There was a silent pause, during which I felt my heart sink to the floor. No, through the floor and into the boiler room in the basement.

Then a loud buzzer went off. "*Incorrect*," Brandon said. "Your sister said you'd prefer a shopping trip to Beverly Hills!"

Jessica turned and glared at me. "I'm not that shallow!"

"So that would be zero points," Brandon said, punching a number into the scoreboard above his head. A large zero appeared on the screen, and the Eights were all smiling as if they'd already won.

"For the Eights, let's go to Gretchen. Gretchen, if you could go anyplace in the world you wanted to, where would you go?" Brandon asked. "And for your information, Julia answered this question for you in the first round."

Gretchen looked at Julia, then back at Brandon. "If I could go anywhere, there's a trip I've been just dying to take."

I started to smile. So they weren't going to get the first one right either. Gretchen sounded as if she had plans to travel somewhere very far away.

"More than anything, I want to go to the Mall of

America," Gretchen said. "It's kind of a dream of mine."

The Eights all cheered as a bell rang to indicate a correct answer, and a "10" glowed in red on the scoreboard above the stage. Next to me, I heard Jessica practically growling. "The Mall of America? What kind of an answer is that? What kind of a question is that? Not like she had to define happiness or anything," she grumbled, "which is only the hardest question in the world."

Brandon cleared his throat. "Next question. Ellen, if you were being shipped off to a desert island and there were only one thing you could bring, what would it be?"

Ellen pondered the question. "This is hard. Why am I being shipped off, anyway?"

Brandon looked exasperated. "That doesn't really matter. Let's say you robbed a bank. The important thing is, what would you take?"

"Mmm . . . how long will I be there?" Ellen asked.

"A long, *long* time," Brandon said, growing increasingly irritated even though the audience thought Ellen's answers were hilarious.

"Then I'm going to say . . . food," Ellen said. "Nonperishable items, like canned goods and rice cakes and stuff like that."

The buzzer seemed to sound even louder the second time it went off. Amanda and the other Eights were grinning from ear to ear. "Lila thought you'd bring your CD player. Sorry, Unicorns."

Not as sorry as we are, I thought. If the Eights got the next question right, we'd be way behind.

"Susan, you're next." Brandon turned to the Eights' counter. "You can increase your lead by quite a bit if you get this one right."

"No kidding," Jessica muttered.

"Susan, what's your idea of the perfect date? Don't be too specific, just the basics," Brandon prompted.

Susan smiled. "Well, this is kind of embarrassing, but I kind of have a thing for basketball players."

That stupid bell must have rung for an entire minute. UNICORNS: 0; EIGHTS: 20. I crossed my fingers when Brandon asked Mary the same question he'd just asked Susan.

"Actually, I don't have any idea of the perfect date," Mary said. "I mean, I don't have a list or anything. He just has to be a nice person."

I don't need to say anything about what happened next, do I? Kristin from the Eights got the next question right, so they had thirty points, Evie missed the one about her prized possession—she said it was her grandmother's thrift store, not her violin—and then, to top it all off, Erica said she couldn't *possibly* go on a trip with just one suitcase. It would have to be a huge trunk.

When we went to the next commercial so we could separate for the second round, we all just looked at one anther as if it were the end of the world. It *felt* like it, that was for sure.

"How can we be losing so badly?" Mandy complained. "How? I don't get it."

"We just must not be thinking clearly," Mary said. "This time, when you guys go off stage, we'll really try to answer the way we think you would. So just think like yourselves and it'll be right."

"The only way we can win is if they get *none* right and we get them *all* right," Jessica whined.

"No, the last question's worth twenty-five points, right? We can still beat them, it won't be easy, but it's possible," Evie said, sounding a little hopeful. "We'll just try to stare them down, intimidate them somehow."

That didn't seem very likely, especially now that the Eights had all the confidence and momentum—and we had none.

"Come on, you guys," Maria urged. "We're not going to lose! You have to think positively!"

I smiled. "Maria's right. We'll never get any points if we get all depressed now. Let's *make* ourselves get the next four right—no matter what."

I sat in the soundproof room—which turned out to be just a noisy equipment room in the basement—and thought about how I would answer any question Brandon threw at me. I thought about how Jessica believes in ESP, and so I even tried to read Brandon's mind. Nothing. (Maybe that's because there wasn't much on his mind. He did seem to be more style than substance. It was as if he couldn't function if he didn't have his index cards.)

After about five minutes, Dan came to get us to bring us back onto the stage. No one said anything as we filed back upstairs. I think everyone was still in a state of shock over what had happened in the first round.

Evie, Ellen, Mary, and Jessica were smiling when we met them back at the counter, so I figured the questions must have been a little easier, or at least more straightforward, this time around. *Maybe it's astrological signs*, I thought hopefully, *or favorite foods*.

I couldn't even pay attention to the Eights. All I knew was that they got the first question wrong, which gave us a chance to catch up.

Everyone looked eagerly at Mandy as Brandon asked her the first question of the second round. "Mandy, Mary's told me what *she* thinks your favorite sport is. Now, let's hear if she was right." Brandon smiled. "Here's the perfect opportunity for the Unicorns to get right back into the game."

"Thanks for pointing out the obvious," Jessica whispered to me.

"Favorite sport?" Mandy asked. "Umm . . . well . . ." So much for confidence. "Baseball?"

Bzzzzz. "No, she said it was soccer." Brandon shrugged. "Sorry, girls. But there is still hope. Remember, our last question's worth twenty-five points."

"Soccer? I hate soccer!" Mandy cried.

"You do not," Mary retorted. "You go to practically every game."

Brandon asked Erica something about Amanda, which she got right. Now it was *fifty* to zero. Ellen didn't get Lila's "most embarrassing moment ever" right, and Evie missed the question for Maria. Naturally, the Eights kept going strong, finishing up with a correct answer on the bonus question. Meanwhile, all the Unicorns were snapping at one another, getting angry at one another for not giving the right answers when it was obvious what they were.

When Brandon turned to me last, I told myself I absolutely had to think like Jessica and get the final bonus question right. At least then we'd have some pride left—the score would be ninety-five to twenty-five instead of ninety-five to zero.

"OK, Elizabeth. Here we go. I still have faith in you Unicorns." Brandon picked up the next index card. "On a scale from one to ten, with ten being the highest, how did Jessica say you would rate the food at your school cafeteria?"

What does that have to do with friendship? I wanted to ask—no, yell. During the whole show, the questions had been pretty lame, but this one—how was I supposed to pick the right number when I had ten options? I stared at Brandon to let him know how angry I was.

He didn't seem to notice. That's when I heard it. Jessica was tapping her foot against the floor, stopping, then tapping again. She was giving me the answer! I wasn't going to cheat, on top of everything else, so I blocked the noise out of my mind. I pictured different dishes at the cafeteria: desserts . . . macaroni and cheese . . . gluey tuna casserole. . . . Jessica had heard me complain about how the brownies weren't fudgy enough, but she also knew I liked the salad bar.

"Elizabeth? We're almost out of time," Brandon urged me.

I took a deep breath. "A four."

The buzzer for a wrong answer coincided with the theme song bursting out of the speakers.

"I said three! Didn't you hear me tapping?" Jessica yelled above the noise.

"Jessica, I wasn't about to cheat!" I yelled back, while Dan, Brandon, and the studio audience loudly applauded the winners.

"And with a final score of ninety-five to zero, the Eight Times Eight Club proves that they are truly best friends," Brandon said with a phony smile.

"As if rating cafeteria food has anything to do with friendship!" Mandy complained into the microphone.

"Sore loser," Amanda shot back.

"Unicorn Club, don't despair!" Brandon said. "We have some lovely consolation prizes for you. First, some hair products for each of you." Dan distributed tiny plastic packs of shampoo and soap to each of us. "And besides that, a gift certificate for dinner for eight at Weird Wally's!"

"Weird Wally's?" Lila complained. "I haven't been there since I was six!" Weird Wally's is a burger place that has tons of games and toys to keep kids occupied, and clowns for waiters. I mean, real clowns, with makeup, red noses, and big shoes.

"And for the winning team . . ."

The Eights started cheering all over again. Jessica put her hand over her eyes.

"Each team member will receive a twenty-five-dollar gift certificate to CDs Plus, a new music store in downtown Sweet Valley!" Brandon announced.

"They get new CDs, and we get hamburgers." Jessica shook her head. "Elizabeth, if you'd only—"

"Me? Why is it my fault?" I snapped. "You didn't get anything right, either."

"Amanda? How do you feel?" Brandon asked. "In thirty seconds or less."

"I feel great. I'm especially glad we won today, because it makes me feel as if being in a club and having such good friends is, like, one of the most important things in life," Amanda said, and the studio audience clapped.

"A noble sentiment, to be sure. Well, folks, that's it for this week on *Best Friends*," Brandon said. He winked at the camera. "Tune in next week to see a new group of contestants answer the question: How well do you *really* know your friends?"

I glanced at everyone as we halfheartedly wandered off the stage toward the exit. *Not very well, I guess*, I thought. Not only did Jessica and I not understand each other, she'd tried to cheat—and then yelled at me for not reading her mind! I never thought she'd turn her back on me that way.

"Oh, and by the way, we'll see you in the cafeteria tomorrow at noon," Amanda said with a smile as we walked past her toward the door. "We're really looking forward to it."

" 'Puff the magic dragon . . .' " Marcy sang.

"Hey, someone bring a videocamera to school tomorrow," Julia said.

I thought I'd have to restrain Lila or Jessica from punching them, but they both looked so down, they hardly even responded. "Yeah, whatever," Jessica muttered.

Ten

I was surprised that we could even ride home in the same cars together, everyone was so mad at one another. Jessica and I weren't speaking. Mandy was angry with Mary. Even Evie, who never has a bad word to say about anybody (well, except maybe Amanda in the past week or so), was rude to Maria when she said good-bye to her.

My parents seemed down, too. They kept trying to cheer us up, but it wasn't working. What could they say? They couldn't honestly tell us we'd done well or tried our hardest. There was just no explanation that I could find for our having bombed—except that we weren't as good friends as we thought we were.

Steven was waiting for us in the kitchen when we got home. *Uh-oh,* I thought. *Here it comes.* He never misses a chance to tease us when it's at all possible.

"Hey," he said, lightly punching me on the arm. "Tough break." He kind of smiled and kind of looked sad at the same time.

I couldn't believe Steven was being so nice. I started to say something, but I couldn't get the words out. Before I knew what was happening, I had burst into tears, run upstairs and into my room, and slammed my bedroom door behind me.

I lay down on my bed and pressed my face into the pillow. I wanted to forget that afternoon had ever happened. I'd never felt so let down before—not just because we had lost, but because of the way we'd lost. Instead of trying to deal with the show together, everyone had turned on everyone else and started accusing everyone else of messing up, when really it wasn't anyone's fault.

Maybe it was *my* fault for trying to get us on the show in the first place. What was it I'd written in that letter? Something about how my friends were always there for me?

I'd just burst out crying in front of Jessica, and she hadn't even come upstairs yet to see if I was OK. Was that being a friend?

We'd grilled one another on every detail of one another's lives, and we'd told ourselves over and over again how great we were. But when Brandon started asking those stupid questions and we couldn't get them right, all of a sudden it was as if we weren't friends anymore. No one said, "Hey, too bad that question was rotten." Instead, it was, "How can you not know that, you idiot?"

Maybe we did know a lot about one another. And maybe the show hadn't given us the opportunity to prove that. But what did knowing things have to do with being a good friend? So what if Lila was a Taurus? So what if Ellen loved banana-chocolate-chip ice cream? Those things didn't mean anything. We could have missed every question and then some, and still acted like best friends. We could have supported one another. But instead my own sister, my identical twin, whom I felt closer to than anybody on earth, thought I was a failure for not knowing how to rate the cafeteria food.

I remembered a line from the letter I'd sent to Brandon. "I think friends are one of the most important things in life." At the moment, I didn't know if any of us could even be friends anymore. I knew we hadn't lost on *Best Friends* because we weren't best friends. But then, the *way* we'd lost made me wonder if we really were.

Best friends didn't yell at each other. Best friends stayed a group, no matter what. One for all, all for one. As I lay there on my bed, I thought, *It's more like one for one. Every Unicorn for herself.*

Bzzzzzzzzz.

When my alarm went off the next morning, I thought it was the buzzer from *Best Friends.* I pulled the covers over my head and tried to go back to sleep.

That's when I remembered: the bet.

If I went to school, I'd have to sing "Puff the

Magic Dragon." Maybe it was a good day to stay home sick. Then I thought about everyone else in the club. If I didn't show, they'd have to do it without me, which wasn't really fair. Unless we all stayed home. But eventually, we'd have to go back, and the Eights would be waiting for us.

I sat up in bed and groaned. Not only would we have to sing, we'd have to face Amanda, not to mention everyone in school who had seen us on the show. And thanks to our banners and all the boasting going around at school, there was probably not one person who hadn't seen it.

This was going to be one of the longest days of my life.

I bumped into Jessica as she was coming out of the bathroom. "Watch where you're going," she snapped.

"Watch where *you're* going," I replied. I wasn't about to take the blame for everything.

She stared at me for a second, then stuck her nose in the air and walked off down the hall to her room.

Make that *the* longest day of my life.

I didn't talk to anyone when I got to school. Instead I made sure I got there right before the final bell, and then I just sort of slunk into homeroom, hoping no one would talk to me. They didn't. Then it hit me: Who would want to talk to me, after yesterday? I might as well have had a sign on my forehead: LOSER.

When I saw the other Unicorns in some of my classes, nobody said anything to anybody else except a curt "Hi," and then they'd turn away and start talking to someone else, a non-Unicorn. I had social studies class with Mandy and Jessica. When I walked in, they weren't even *sitting* next to each other, and we'd had the same seats all year!

"Hi, Mandy," I said, pausing by her desk.

"Hi," she said, only glancing up for a second.

"Can I ask you something?"

Mandy shrugged.

"What are we going to do about the bet?" Out of the corner of my eye, I saw Jessica watching us.

"Beats me," Mandy said, shrugging again.

What kind of an answer is that? I wanted to say. "So . . . we're not going through with it?" I asked.

"I don't know. You'll have to ask everyone else," Mandy said.

Mandy was the president, the one who could get along with anybody on the planet, and she wasn't even talking to anyone?

I didn't know what to do. I felt so nervous after talking to her—or trying to talk to her—that when I sat down at my desk, I was shaking all over.

When lunchtime came, I headed to the cafeteria, the same as usual. First, because I was hungry. And second, because I don't think there's much point in trying to get out of things when you can't.

I glanced around, but I didn't see any of the other Unicorns in line or sitting anywhere—especially not in our usual spot, the Unicorner. I was about to get in line when Charlie Cashman started banging a knife against a glass to get everyone's attention. He was standing in the middle of the cafeteria with Rick Hunter, Todd Wilkins, and Aaron Dallas.

"Attention, ladies and gentlemen," Charlie said. "While you're eating lunch, we have a special entertainment feature for you."

I started to shake. Were they introducing the Unicorns? So we could sing "Puff the Magic Dragon"? Was I going to be the only one there, deserted by everyone? They were probably all sitting outside eating their sandwiches, while I was left to defend the dignity of our club. What nerve!

I glanced around nervously. If I tried to sneak out, Charlie would see me for sure. So I sank into a chair behind a table of tall eighth-grade boys and hoped no one would notice me.

"As you all know, one of the hottest new shows on TV is *Best Friends*," Todd said, standing beside Charlie.

I drummed my fingers against the table. I was so nervous, I thought I was going to pass out. I pictured myself standing up there, in front of everyone, singing. My quavering voice would be heard by everyone—and laughed at by everyone.

"Some of us weren't lucky enough to see yesterday's show," Todd continued, "so we thought we'd have our own show right here."

Ken Matthews, who's tall and blond, with blue eyes, stood up next. "Hello, sports fans. It's time to ask yourself: Are you really Worst Enemies?" He winked, perfectly imitating Brandon Blitzen's smooth and sort of sleazy manner.

Everyone in the cafeteria started cheering. I saw Amanda and the Eights laughing and yelling. I was glad I'd managed to avoid them so far all day. Sitting there, I felt a little like a fugitive, hiding out at my own school.

Charlie Cashman is definitely one of the most obnoxious boys at school, and I had a horrible feeling I knew what he and his friends were up to.

"OK, now, our two teams today are Todd and Rick, and Aaron and Charlie. Aaron, we'll start with you. If you could go anywhere in the world, where would it be?" Ken asked, grinning.

"Well, umm . . ." Aaron stared off into space. "You know, I think I'd like to go to a desert island. I hear the shopping's really good there."

Everyone laughed. I felt my face turn pink and wondered if Ellen was anywhere around. She'd be dying, if she was.

"And now a follow-up question. If you did go to a desert island, Aaron, what would you bring?" Ken asked.

"Gee, that's hard. I don't know, like, salad dressing, I guess, 'cause I'd probably be eating lots of plants and stuff," Aaron said, imitating Ellen to a T. The boys in front of me burst out laughing.

"OK, now. Charlie. If Todd could go anywhere, where would he go?" Ken asked. "Remember, you need to match his answer."

"This is hard. Can you repeat the question?" Charlie asked.

All five boys made a loud buzzing noise at once.

"Sorry, that's wrong," Ken said, winking at the crowd.

People sitting around me were actually *howling* with laughter. I'm usually pretty able to laugh at myself, but this was above and beyond anything I'd ever had to deal with—not to mention the fact that I was having to deal with it all by myself.

"Now, Todd and Rick, it's your turn. Seeing as how you're twins, I think this is going to be a cinch for you," Ken said. I slumped even farther down in my chair. "Todd, if Rick had to eat one thing in this cafeteria, *what* would it be?"

Todd tapped his fingers against his chin. "Probably the tuna casserole. Or maybe the macaroni and cheese. Maybe he'd just have a Coke. You know, I really don't know."

I felt my face turning bright red as people watched the boys, then glanced over at me, then back at them. Even my ears were burning, and I wished I'd worn my hair down, the way Jessica does. Or else I could have combed it completely over my face, so it wouldn't be so obvious that I was feeling totally humiliated. How could they be so mean? For a second I thought maybe the Eights had put them up to this, but then I realized we'd probably struck everyone as pathetic yesterday when we didn't manage to get even one point.

I couldn't take it anymore. I pushed back my

chair and started to walk out of the cafeteria. I was halfway to the door when Amanda got up from her table and approached me.

Amanda didn't say anything at first. She just got close enough to make me think she was going to. Then she hummed a few bars of "Puff the Magic Dragon."

"I know, I know," I said with a loud, exasperated sigh. Nothing like having someone rub salt in an open wound, but I wasn't exactly surprised.

"So . . . where is everyone?" Amanda asked.

I glanced over at the Unicorner, which was completely deserted. It should have had a real-estate sign on it saying: VACANT—FOR RENT. "I guess everyone was too busy today," I said with a shrug, trying to sound casual.

"But what about your song?" Amanda asked. "We *did* make a bet."

"I know," I said. "And we're going to follow through with it. Monday," I said. "Don't worry." Then I walked out of the cafeteria before she could say anything else.

Jessica and I still weren't talking by the time we got home from school that afternoon. I couldn't believe it. I couldn't remember the last time that had happened. I wasn't mad at her, except that I thought she should apologize for snapping at me about the cafeteria question. And I wasn't going to make it easy on her and make the first move.

On the other hand, I wasn't exactly looking forward to the weekend if it meant living in the same house with my sister and not talking to her for two days. Then I remembered that the day-care center was having an open house on Saturday—tomorrow—which we were all supposed to go to. Not that it was required, because we weren't employees or anything. It was just that last weekend at the football game we'd all talked about going. It would be a chance to spend some time with the kids, meet the parents we hadn't met yet, and maybe meet some new kids. A real family day.

Then I wondered if anyone would show up, the way things were going. I still wanted to. I wasn't going to let Allison think I didn't keep my word. But what if we *all* showed up? Then what? It would be so awkward. We'd have to talk eventually.

I decided to call Mandy. She hadn't been very pleasant to me that morning, but out of everyone, I thought she might be the most willing to make the first (or second, since I was calling her) move. And she was the president, after all.

"Hi, Mandy," I said when she answered the phone. I had dragged the hall phone into my room and shut the door, so Jessica wouldn't hear me.

"Elizabeth?" she asked, as if she were surprised to hear from me.

"Yeah, it's me," I said. "I want to talk to you about something."

"Sure. Go ahead," Mandy said. She didn't sound very encouraging, but I wasn't going to let that stop me.

"Mandy, I want you to call an emergency meeting of the Unicorns," I said.

"I'm the president, Elizabeth," Mandy said. "And it's up to me to decide when to call emergency meetings." She didn't sound like herself at all. She sounded downright snooty. There was a long moment of silence, and I wondered if she was going to hang up on me. Then she said, "Well, they're having that open-house thing over at the day-care center tomorrow morning. We did promise the kids and Mrs. Willard we'd be there."

"What time should I show up?" I asked.

"How about ten?" Mandy suggested.

"OK. Do you want me to help you call everyone?" I asked.

"No." Mandy sighed, sounding exasperated, as if she were angry with me. "*I'll* do it."

Eleven

Ellen walked into the day-care center on Saturday morning looking as though she'd just stepped out of a tornado. Her hair was as messy as if she hadn't been brushing it in the last few days, and she had her sweater on inside out.

Maria had her rattiest jeans on, the ones with all the holes, the ones she's had forever. Even Lila didn't look that good. She usually looks beautiful no matter what she's wearing. Not today. She had on some old gray leggings and a big, baggy sweatshirt that might have belonged to her father when he was in college.

We were sitting in Mrs. Willard's office, which she was nice enough to let us use. She was busy outside, setting up picnic tables and punch bowls for the open house. "You have half an hour, girls," she'd told us. "After that I need my office back so I can meet with parents."

After everyone arrived, it was incredibly awkward. We were crowded into this little office, and no one was really saying anything. I just listened to the clock on the wall ticking away the minutes. There was something really . . . *off* about everyone. Then it hit me: None of us was wearing any purple—not anywhere!

"Don't we even want to be Unicorns anymore?" I blurted, before Mandy even had a chance to call the meeting to order.

No one said anything at first. They all looked at me kind of funny, as if they were surprised I was the one who had said something. "What do you mean?" Jessica finally asked, in a timid-sounding voice. She smiled at me for the first time since Thursday. It was only a teeny-tiny smile, but I saw it.

"Well, for one thing, no one's wearing any purple, as far as I can tell," I said. "Since when don't we wear purple? And how about yesterday, when no one showed up in the cafeteria? And no one even told me that no one *else* was showing up? I can't believe you guys all left me there by myself!" I complained. "Where did you all go?"

"*We* didn't go anywhere, at least not together," Mandy said. "I sat outside on the lawn and ate a bag of potato chips I brought from home. There was no way I was going into that cafeteria with Amanda waiting for me to sing."

"Why didn't you tell me that in social studies class?" I asked.

Mandy didn't say anything for a minute. "I don't know. I guess that was pretty lousy of me. I was just so miserable, I wasn't thinking about anybody else."

"It's something that's going around," I commented. We had all been acting selfish since yesterday. It was like the Unicorn Club had vanished into thin air, and all I was left with was a bunch of purple clothes.

"I'm sorry, Elizabeth, but I didn't know what to do," Maria admitted. "I just knew I didn't want to see Amanda and those awful Eights."

"Yeah, I wasn't going to give her the chance to rub our noses in it," Jessica said. "But I heard the boys were making fun of us."

"Yeah, it was pretty bad," I said. "But you know what was even worse? When I left, there was nobody sitting in the Unicorner. Nobody."

Mandy sighed. "Well, what are we going to do? I mean, we can't just go back into school on Monday like nothing happened. I'm embarrassed to show my face! And it's not going to get any easier."

"I know. I'm embarrassed, too," Evie said. "But we have to eat lunch *some*time."

Everyone laughed a little at that. It helped lighten the mood in the room.

"You guys, we can't let one dumb show ruin our whole year," I said. "I mean, we've been having a *great* year, up until now. I don't want to spend the seventh grade in hiding because of some dumb game show against the Eights."

"It's not just the show," Lila said angrily. It was the first thing she'd said. "Now we have to humiliate ourselves all over again because of the dumb bet we made." She glared right at Jessica.

"You guys all wanted to make that bet!" Jessica protested, jumping out of her chair. "OK, sure, it was my idea at first, but you didn't have to go along with me."

"Jessica's right, you know. We didn't have to make the bet, but we did—we *all* did. I mean, I'm the one who suggested the stupid song to sing, because I was so sure we'd win, but we didn't, and now we have to live with it," I said. Jessica smiled at me again.

"Why didn't we win?" Mary asked. "I've been thinking about it ever since Thursday."

"OK, first of all, those questions were not what we expected," Maria said.

"Not only that, they were moronic," Jessica said. "Watching the show, I never realized that before, but they are!"

"It's like that last question about the food," Mandy said to me. "I mean, you'd have to be a mind reader to pick the same number as Jessica."

"And I couldn't read Lila's mind if my life depended on it," Ellen said.

"And I couldn't figure out what you'd say, either," Lila said. "Or how you think, or what you'll show up wearing to school one day, or—"

"That's exactly it!" Evie suddenly cried. "We couldn't have won, because we're all so different. We don't think alike."

"You're right," Mandy said. "I mean, when's the last time all of us agreed on anything? Not that we don't get along, but we do argue about stuff a lot."

"That's because we're all different," Mary said. "For one, we dress differently." She pointed to her preppie khakis, oxford-cloth shirt, and brown penny loafers, then to Mandy's bowling shirt with the name "Ralph" stitched across the pocket, blue-and-white-striped overalls, and saddle shoes.

"And then there's the Eights," I said. "They dress alike, look alike—"

"Act mean alike—"

"They got those answers right because they *all* like to date basketball players, and they *all* want to go to the Mall of America," Jessica declared. "That's probably what they sit around and talk about!"

"It's like all eight of them are sharing one brain," Mary said.

"Sounds like a science-fiction movie," Ellen said, laughing.

"I don't mean it in a mean way, like they're not smart, because they are," Mary said. "They just happen to be . . . like Xerox copies of each other sometimes."

"Which works perfectly on a game show when the host is Mr. Plastic Personality," Jessica complained. "Oooh, I hate that man. Did you see the way he looked at us when he gave us our stupid parting gifts? Like we were pathetic or something. We just lost, that's all."

"Yeah, but we've been *acting* pretty pathetic," I replied. "Haven't we?"

Mandy nodded. "Yeah. Just because we lost, we shouldn't disappear from the face of the earth. I mean, it was a fifty-fifty chance. Someone had to lose."

"And just because we lost, that doesn't mean we don't know what it's like to be best friends," Mary said. "The best thing we could do now is something to show everyone we still believe in ourselves, even if they don't."

"So how are we going to do that, with this dumb song we have to sing on Monday?" Jessica asked.

"Well, I think I have a plan," I said. "It's going to take some work, though."

"Let's hear it," Mandy said, and everyone leaned a little closer to me, as if I were about to tell them a juicy secret.

"Can we get Amanda kicked out of school somehow?" Ellen asked. "Is it something like that?"

"No, not quite," I said. "OK, the bet is that the losers have to perform 'Puff the Magic Dragon.' But, we never said *which* 'Puff the Magic Dragon.'"

"Isn't there only one?" Lila asked.

"Sure, now there is," I said. "But we could make up a new version, couldn't we?"

"You mean . . . we could rewrite it?" Ellen asked.

"Right. We could change it," I said.

"And we could make it hip!" Mandy exclaimed. "We could make it a dance number—"

"That's a fantastic idea!" Jessica leapt off of her

chair. "We can make it really cool, so instead of them showing us up, we'll show *them* up."

"Exactly." I smiled.

"It'll take a lot of work, maybe even all weekend," Lila said.

"We need someone to write the lyrics, someone to coordinate the dancing . . ." Mandy started making a list.

"There *are* eight of us," Maria said. "If we all work together, we can come up with a great routine."

"And get our reputation back," Lila said.

"Do we really have to work together?" Jessica asked me.

I nodded. "Definitely."

"Good," she said. Then she gave me a little hug.

We spent the first part of the afternoon hanging out with the kids at the day-care center. Then we went over to Ellen's house to work on our song. She has a big basement with a finished rec room and a stereo. She and Maria went through all her CDs, trying to find a good dance tune we could use for our background music. Mary wasn't crazy about dancing, so we decided she could introduce us to the crowd and be the MC. Evie turned out to be sort of an electronics whiz, so we got her to agree to man the tape player we'd bring in.

Then it came down to an argument between Lila and Jessica, as usual. They both wanted the lead singing role.

"I have an idea," Mandy said. She was going to coordinate our outfits for the performance. "Tell me if this will work. We can write a rap, and you guys can alternate saying the lines."

"OK," Jessica said. "That's fine with me."

"There's only one problem," Lila said. "We need someone to write the lines in the first place—I can't ad lib a rap."

All of a sudden, everyone was looking at me. "Oh, no," I said. "Why do I have to write everything all the time—"

"Elizabeth!" Mary cried, her hands on her hips. "Don't you even want to be a Unicorn?" She grinned, and everyone laughed.

Since my writing that letter to Brandon had gotten us into this trouble to start with, I guess it was only fair that I write something else to try to get us out of trouble. "Ellen, do you have some paper and a pen I could use?" I asked.

"Go, Elizabeth!" Maria shouted.

Twelve

When we walked up to school on Monday morning, the Eights were standing on the front steps, as if they'd been waiting there all night for us. Maybe all weekend. I wouldn't have been surprised if they had. They were like vultures, circling and waiting for the kill. (OK, maybe that's getting a little carried away.)

"How was your weekend?" Amanda asked us, in a phony cheerful voice.

"You know, I had the best weekend I've had in a long time," Jessica said with a smile. "Really, incredibly great."

"Yeah, sure," Julia said under her breath.

"I bet you're excited about what happens at noon today," Marcy said.

"What would that be?" Lila asked, looking puzzled.

"Your musical number?" Amanda said. "Or did you forget?"

"No, we didn't forget," Mary said. "Actually, we were practicing all weekend. See, Maria even brought our background music." She pointed to the tape player in Maria's hand.

"Yeah, we really had to struggle to get the harmony right," Maria added. Then she sang a few lines of the original "Puff the Magic Dragon."

"It's a tough song to learn," Evie explained, sounding very serious.

Amanda grinned. "Well, you guys were the ones who came up with the song. Maybe you should have thought about it more, before you made that bet."

"Yeah, maybe." I sighed. "Oh, well. We have to go through with it sooner or later." I shrugged and tried to look distressed.

"Well, don't forget to show up or anything," Amanda said. "I have my introduction all planned."

"Don't worry, we'll be there," Jessica told Amanda, patting her on the shoulder.

As we walked into school, all eight of us broke up into laughter. "I hope this works as well as it did in rehearsal yesterday," Mandy said. She was carrying a bag of baseball caps she'd made especially for us. They were purple with green dragons on the front of them. We were going to wear them sideways.

"It will," Jessica said confidently. "And this time, I mean it. We're ready."

"Maybe we should have invited Brandon," I said, "so he can see we aren't losers after all."

"Like he would even know the difference," Lila said. "Not to mention the fact that he wouldn't even get the lyrics."

"Did you memorize them last night?" I asked her.

"Like you wouldn't believe. My dad kept coming into my room to see what all the noise was. He thought I was talking to myself," Lila said.

"Steven thought I was going to start my own rap band, and every time he came down the hall, he'd yell like he was trying to imitate me," Jessica said. "And believe me, you do not want to hear Steven try to rap."

I laughed. "Are you guys sure you don't want to start a band? I mean, Unicorn Ice kind of has a nice ring to it."

Lila shook her head. "Stick to writing, OK?"

Then the bell rang and we all hurried off to our lockers, calling, "See you at noon!"

Amanda stood on a chair in the middle of the cafeteria. We were all hovering just outside the door, except for Evie, who was inside setting up the music, and Mary, who was our other stage manager. I made a last-minute adjustment to Jessica's dragon baseball cap.

"Attention!" Amanda yelled. "I have something important to say. Today's lunch is very special because—"

"It's actually edible!" Charlie called out.

"No . . ." Amanda said slowly. "Because the Unicorn Club is here to entertain you, with their performance of a folk classic, 'Puff the Magic Dragon.'" Most of the kids I could see either groaned, complained, or kept eating. "Unicorns, take it away!" Amanda cried, jumping off her chair and going back to the table where the rest of the Eights were sitting. They all laughed or snickered.

Evie pressed the play button, and loud dance music boomed out of the small speakers. We went into the cafeteria one by one, single file, dancing from side to side. Already I could tell we had people's attention. I like to be modest, but let's face it, we are all pretty good dancers.

In the middle of the cafeteria, Ellen, Maria, Mandy, and I fanned out behind Lila and Jessica. We danced in syncopated moves for about thirty seconds, and then Jessica and Lila started to sing, alternating each line.

"Puff the magic dragon was a sad old thing!
He couldn't dance and he couldn't sing!
He didn't know how to bust a move—
Let's just say, he wasn't in the groove!
Puff! P-p-p-puff!"

We lunged from side to side, while Lila and Jessica repeated the last line. They actually sounded as if they knew what they were doing, but every time I got a glimpse of Lila in her sunglasses and sideways baseball cap, I had to try not to crack up. If her father could have seen her!

> "Puff the magic dragon lived in L.A.
> He drove around a lot in his Chevrolet
> The car was too small, his tail was too long
> But he powered through traffic by singing this song
> Puff! P-p-p-puff!"

By the end of the second verse, some other people in the cafeteria were actually standing and dancing with us. Everyone else was either laughing (which was OK, we wanted them to laugh) or just watching us. A few kids pointed and shook their heads.

> "One day Puff went to high school
> They told him breathing fire just wasn't cool
> But he had to be different, he didn't care
> He was a dragon just full of hot air!
> Puff! P-p-p-puff!"

When we finished—the whole thing lasted only about four minutes—I looked over at the Eights to see what they thought. Amanda had such a big frown on her face, she actually looked like a mean dragon. People in the cafeteria were cheering and whistling for us as the music ended. We took a group bow. Some people were still laughing.

"Encore!" someone shouted.

"Sorry, this is a one-time-only performance," Jessica said.

Amanda stood up, glared at us, then turned and stormed out of the cafeteria. Marcy followed her, but Julia smiled at us and even clapped a little bit. "Nice job," she said. "I wouldn't have thought of that."

"Yeah, you guys are pretty original," Carmen commented, looking as if she wasn't sure if that was a good thing or not.

Then Evie put on another dance tape, and we bopped out of the cafeteria in single file.

"We did it!" I cried, giving Jessica a high-five outside in the hallway. "You guys were great."

We were so busy celebrating, we didn't notice Mr. Clark coming out of the lunchroom until he was right in front of us. He tapped Mandy on the shoulder. "Excuse me," he said.

"Oh, hi, Mr. Clark. What's up?" Mandy asked.

"Oh, no! I completely forgot!" I said. "We were supposed to meet you on Friday, to give you the money. I'm sorry."

"You forgot?" Mr. Clark said.

"Well, Friday was kind of a bad day for us," Jessica explained. "We really weren't thinking clearly."

"Yes, I understand how it could have slipped your mind, with the game show and everything," Mr. Clark said. "But listen, that isn't—"

"But of course, we *do* understand our responsibility!" Ellen piped in. "We do need to meet with you."

"Yes, but—" Mr. Clark began again.

"How about tomorrow after school—like at two-thirty?" Mary suggested.

"All right, but there's something I should tell you," Mr. Clark said.

"Don't worry, Mr. Clark. You don't have to tell us twice. We've got this whole thing straightened out," Mandy said, patting him on the arm.

"That was a very interesting performance in the cafeteria yesterday." Mr. Clark tapped a pen against his desk. It was after school on Tuesday afternoon. "Very interesting." He looked a little concerned, like maybe we had all lost our minds or something. "And by the way, I'm sorry about the game show."

"It's OK. We're over it," Mandy said. "Actually, this week's going great for us."

"It is?" Mr. Clark looked puzzled.

"Sure," Mary said. "And the great news is, we have some money for you."

"You do?" Now he really seemed surprised.

"We started an odd-jobs service—maybe you saw our flyers around town?" Evie asked. "Well, we got tons of work. More than we could handle, actually."

"And we did every odd job there is," I added, "even taking someone's ferret for a walk in the park."

"Don't remind me." Lila shuddered. "I didn't like those animals before, and I still don't."

I took the envelope of cash out of my pocket and

put it on Mr. Clark's desk. "There's seventy-five dollars," I said. "Now we only owe you two hundred and twenty-five."

Ellen groaned, and Mr. Clark looked over at her distractedly. "Sorry. It just sounds like a lot."

Mr. Clark didn't say anything. He was looking inside the envelope carefully, as if a springy snake were going to jump out of it. He counted the money, then set the envelope back down. "Girls, I am very impressed. Very."

I turned to Jessica and smiled. There were some things we could do right, after all.

"And you know what? I've learned something important from this experience," Mr. Clark went on. He stood up and began pacing around his office with his hands behind his back.

"That we're reliable?" Mandy hinted.

"That we keep our word?" Maria asked.

"Well, those things, too," he acknowledged with a smile. "But the big thing is, I've decided I don't want to get a new hairpiece, after all."

"*What?*" Ellen practically shrieked. "You mean that I scrubbed Mr. Granger's disgusting bathtub for nothing?"

"Does this mean you're going with the hair-in-a-can solution?" Mandy asked.

"Will you wear hats?" Jessica asked. "Because I think I should tell you, Mr. Clark, I've heard that hats can actually increase hair loss." She looked extremely concerned for a second.

Mr. Clark shook his head. "I'm not going to do

anything. No miracle cures, no sprays or hats."

"You mean . . . you're just going to stay the way you are?" I asked.

Mr. Clark nodded. "Over the past weeks, while I've waited for you to replace my hairpiece, I've realized something. There's nothing really wrong with being bald. In fact, I kind of like the way I look."

"That's great!" Mandy said. "To tell you the truth, we think you look better this way, too."

"Yeah," Ellen said, "more natural."

"So I suppose in a strange sense, I should thank you girls for destroying my original hairpiece. I might never have come to accept my baldness if it weren't for you," Mr. Clark said, smiling at each of us in turn.

"So . . . can we have the money back?" Jessica was staring at the envelope of five-dollar bills on Mr. Clark's desk, looking a little on the obsessed side.

Trust Jessica to get straight to the point, especially if there's any cash involved.

"Well, no," Mr. Clark said.

"Why not?" Lila demanded.

Take it easy, you guys! I wanted to say. It sounded as if we had finally gotten back on Mr. Clark's good side, and now they were going to bug him again.

"Because I've decided to put the money toward another good cause," Mr. Clark said patiently. "As you well know, we've been trying to build a beach volleyball court out back. Well, I'm planning to use this money as a contribution toward that. But don't worry—I'll give you credit. We'll make sure to put all your names on the list of sponsors."

"You don't have to do that," Mandy said. "Just put one name down: the Unicorn Club."

She turned to me and smiled, and then I smiled at Evie and Maria, who were sitting next to me. It was a great feeling, knowing we were really all best friends again.

"Uh, well, I kind of hate to ask, but what about the other two hundred twenty-five? Do you still want that?" Mary asked.

Mr. Clark rubbed his chin and stared out the window. His office was completely silent while we waited for his answer. He was deciding whether we'd spend the next month washing windows, walking ferrets, and sprinkling lawn fertilizer.

Mr. Clark cleared his throat. "Give me twenty-five more and we'll call it even."

"Yes!" Mandy tried to give Mr. Clark a high-five, but he missed her hand, then blushed.

"Thank you so much," Ellen said. "You don't know how much easier this makes my life."

"Well, thanks for showing me what a superficial thing hair is," Mr. Clark said. "If you hadn't come in here with Mr. Styrofoam Man, you might still be working every odd job in town." He grinned.

We were so happy when we left his office, we had already forgotten about the Eights, *Best Friends*, and the fact that we'd rapped in front of the entire school. All I knew was that we'd pulled together once again, and I was in the club I wanted to be in.

As we walked down the corridor, Lila called over her shoulder, "Anyone going over to the day-care center today?" To Mandy, who was walking next to her, she added, "I told Ellie I'd be there, no matter what. She's so cute, just like a little sister."

"I am," I answered, catching up to them.

"Great," Lila said, and we said good-bye to the others and headed for the day-care center.

As we walked, I thought about how attached Ellie had become to Lila. Who would ever have believed that Lila would be so crazy about a little kid? I guess that's why Ellie ran to Lila's house the time she ran away from home. But I'd better let Lila tell that story. . . .

Read all about our next Unicorn adventure in The Unicorn Club #4, Lila's Little Sister.

SIGN UP FOR THE SWEET VALLEY HIGH® FAN CLUB!

Hey, girls! Get all the gossip on Sweet Valley High's® most popular teenagers when you join our fantastic Fan Club! As a member, you'll get all of this really cool stuff:

- Membership Card with your own personal Fan Club ID number
- A Sweet Valley High® Secret Treasure Box
- Sweet Valley High® Stationery
- Official Fan Club Pencil (for secret note writing!)
- Three Bookmarks
- A "Members Only" Door Hanger
- Two Skeins of J. & P. Coats® Embroidery Floss with flower barrette instruction leaflet
- Two editions of *The Oracle* newsletter
- Plus exclusive Sweet Valley High® product offers, special savings, contests, and much more!

Be the first to find out what Jessica & Elizabeth Wakefield are up to by joining the Sweet Valley High® Fan Club for the one-year membership fee of only $6.25 each for U.S. residents, $8.25 for Canadian residents (U.S. currency). Includes shipping & handling.

Send a check or money order (do not send cash) made payable to "Sweet Valley High® Fan Club" along with this form to:

SWEET VALLEY HIGH® FAN CLUB, BOX 3919-B, SCHAUMBURG, IL 60168-3919

NAME_____
(Please print clearly)

ADDRESS_____

CITY_____ STATE _____ ZIP_____
(Required)

AGE _____ BIRTHDAY_____ /_____ /_____

Offer good while supplies last. Allow 6-8 weeks after check clearance for delivery. Addresses without ZIP codes cannot be honored. Offer good in USA & Canada only. Void where prohibited by law.
©1993 by Francine Pascal   LCI-1383-123

Your friends at Sweet Valley
High have had their world
turned upside down!

Meet one person with a power
so evil, so dangerous, that it
could destroy the entire world
of Sweet Valley!

A Night to Remember, the book that starts it all, is followed
by a six book series filled with romance, drama and suspense.

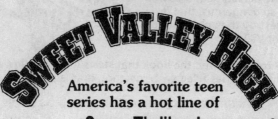